I0548967

The Beasor Chronicles

TRAMPS

T. A. CHASE

Tramps
ISBN # 978-1-78184-535-6
©Copyright T.A. Chase 2012
Cover Art by Posh Gosh ©Copyright August 2012
Interior text design by Claire Siemaszkiewicz
Total-E-Bound Publishing

Published in 2012 by Total-E-Bound Publishing, Think Tank, Ruston Way, Lincoln, LN6 7FL, United Kingdom.

Total-E-Bound Publishing is an imprint of Total-E-Ntwined Limited.

TRAMPS

Dedication

Thanks to my readers for continuing to read my stories and letting me know how much you like them. Thank you to my editor for helping me make the stories I write better.

Chapter One

The noise of the pub hit Chal as he pushed open the door. He grinned and waved as Reagan, the head bouncer, nodded towards the back of the pub. It had been a long two weeks and he wanted to drink himself into a stupor before he went home to sleep.

"Hey, there." A voice rang over the noise from the customers.

Chal looked around, and spied Alden, the owner of the pub and one of Chal's closest friends, motioning to him from the table in the corner. He gestured to the bar, and Alden nodded. By the time he got to the counter, Greta had a mug of ale waiting for him.

"Greta, you're a gem." He saluted her with his glass before drinking the ale without stopping. He set the empty mug back on the counter. "Fill 'er up again."

"A long week?" she asked whilst getting him another ale.

"Yes, and after a couple more of these I'm heading home to sleep for three days or so." He snatched his glass up and turned to head over to where Alden sat.

"You're finally back." Percy, Alden's lover, stood and hugged him.

Wrapping his arm around Percy's waist, he gave him a tight squeeze before winking at Alden.

"You're a lucky bastard, Alden." He let go of Percy to shake Alden's hand.

Alden laughed. "I know. We missed seeing your ugly face around here."

Chal dropped into a chair and set his mug down. He scrubbed his hands over his head. "Man, I've been running around like crazy, trying to find this object my client wanted. I had to flash to three different universes and four different worlds before I found what I was looking for. I'm beat."

"Was it worth it at least?" Percy spoke up from where he sat next to Alden.

"Oh, hell yes." Chal laughed. "I charged him through the nose for all those trips. It might not drain me of power to travel through the universes, but he's one of those Beasors who thinks what I do is something like magic."

"You're such a jerk." Percy reached over and poked Chal in the chest. "I can't believe you took advantage of that man."

"Hey, I never said I was a saint. I have to make a living. Some of us don't have a wealthy business owner as a boyfriend to treat us like a prince," he teased the Gypsy.

"Where is this wealthy boyfriend you're talking about?" Percy made a production of looking around the crowd.

Alden grabbed Percy and yanked him over onto his lap. Chal watched the couple kiss for a few minutes before he grabbed a napkin and scrunched it up, throwing it at them. He laughed when it bounced off Percy's head.

"What the hell?" Percy glared at him.

"Ah, pretty boy, don't worry about it. It was clean, and I didn't come here to watch the two of you make out. Not that it isn't the hottest thing I've seen in a long time. Do you think you could refrain from kissing while I'm here?"

Percy pouted for a second, then he nodded. "I guess we could. It's not like we won't be going upstairs in an hour or so and making love all night long."

Chal groaned as his cock hardened at the thought of Percy and Alden in the midst of making love. He whistled for a waitress to bring him another mug. She dropped it off and he took a sip.

"You're being deliberately cruel, aren't you?" Chal whined. "I haven't had sex in like a month or so."

"Why?" Alden nuzzled Percy's neck.

"I've been busy and just haven't found the time."

Percy snorted while Alden shot Chal a sceptical glance. Chal laughed after he took another drink.

"All right. I could have found the time, if I'd met anyone interesting enough for me to make an effort. There just hasn't been anyone around who's caught my eye." He paused. "Well, except for Steril, though even I know there's nothing but trouble with him."

Alden nodded while Percy gasped.

"Steril is a wonderful person. You shouldn't say things like that about him." Percy glared at Alden when his lover poked him in the side. "Hey, Steril's not here to defend himself, so I have to do it for him."

"I have to say, Chal, I understand what you mean. It seems to me Gypsies and Thieves are some of the highest-maintenance Beasors in the universes."

Alden winked at Chal before Percy punched him in the arm. Chal shook his head.

"Well, you know these pretty boys. They need us to grovel at their feet and tell them how much we love them." Chal finished the rest of his ale and stood. He smiled at his friends. "I'm heading home to sleep for like, three days, or something like that."

"I thought travelling between the universes didn't tire you out?" Alden questioned.

Yawning, Chal shrugged. "It normally doesn't, but doing it constantly without really resting for two weeks or so can wear any Tramp out."

"Got it. Well, why don't you call us when you wake up, and we'll meet up for dinner or something?" Alden stood and slapped Chal on the shoulder.

"Sounds good to me." He leant down and kissed Percy on the cheek. "You're looking good, Percy. I'll talk to you later."

He waved at Reagan as he strolled out of the pub. After grabbing a hover sled, he slid into the back, swiped his credit card to pay, and punched in his address. He leant back against the cushions, closing his eyes. The idea of falling into his bed and pulling the blankets up over his head filled his mind. He really needed some sleep. Then he would see about finding a new job.

Chal must have dozed off because he jolted awake when the sled stopped and the bell chimed, alerting him to his arrival at his destination. He somehow climbed out of the sled and stumbled up the steps to his apartment.

After making sure the door was locked, Chal shuffled into his bedroom, leaving a trail of clothes behind him. He'd pick those up in the morning, or whenever he surfaced next.

* * * *

A constant buzzing burrowed deep under the blanket of sleep covering Chal. Grunting, he opened his eyes and blinked at the ceiling above him. It took him a few minutes to remember where he was.

The buzzing hadn't stopped, and Chal practically fell when he tried to get out of his bed. His feet tangled up in the sheets, causing him to swear while he kicked to remove the fabric wrapped around his ankles.

"Quit pushing the fucking button," Chal shouted, stumbling down the hallway to the front door.

He jerked it open to glare at Percy, who stood there with a rather worried expression on his face.

"What the hell do you want?" Chal snarled, but stepped back to allow Percy inside his apartment.

The Gypsy shook his head. "I was worried about you, jackass. No one's heard from you for three days."

"Really? Well, I did say I'd sleep that long." Chal scrubbed his hand over his face before dropping into the closest chair. "I didn't look at a clock. All I did was get up to hit the bathroom when I needed to, then go right back to bed. I guess I was more tired than I thought."

Percy sat on the arm of the chair and rested his hand on Chal's shoulder. "We didn't think you were serious. Are you okay?"

"Yeah. I'm not usually bothered by all the flashing, but I probably should have rested in between trips." He leaned his head back and stared up at Percy. "Are you really here to make sure I'm all right?"

"Of course. Alden was worried about you as well, but he couldn't get away from the pub at the moment.

I just finished a job in the area, so I thought I'd stop by and make sure you're still alive."

Chal blinked in surprise, and grunted. "I don't think I've ever had anyone come to check on me."

"Don't you have any family who might be worried?" Percy moved from the chair to the couch, sitting gracefully before crossing his legs and studying Chal.

"No." He hesitated, then continued, "Well, I have family, but they never really worried about me, especially since I moved out and started working on my own."

"Hmm…I understand that. Do any of us have a happy family story?" Percy tilted his head, like he was thinking about his own family.

"Maybe not in the past, but I think you and Alden are building your own good memories. How are things going for you?" Chal didn't want to think about his family, or how they'd turned their backs on him because he wasn't interested in improving his status in society.

Percy shrugged. "I'm still meeting with a therapist, and working through my issues. I think we're doing well. I've been working off and on for the past month or so."

"That's good news." Chal's stomach rumbled, and he laughed. "It's probably a good thing you stopped by. I'm pretty sure my stomach thinks my throat's been cut."

"If you want, I can call Alden and have him meet us for dinner?" Percy suggested.

"Sounds like a good idea. Why don't you call him, and I'm going to take a shower? I need to clean up." Chal ran his fingers over the stubble on his chin.

Nodding, Percy pulled out his phone, then hit a button. After standing, Chal headed back to his room where he dug out some clean clothes. He went to the bathroom and turned on the shower. He washed up and shaved, taking care not to cut himself while rushing to get ready. He didn't want Percy to come searching for him.

Percy was standing in front of Chal's bookcase when Chal came back into the living room. Smiling, Percy turned to look at him.

"I didn't realise you could read."

"Ha ha. You're such a smartass. What did you think I did when I was by myself?"

Percy shrugged. "I guess I didn't think you spent a lot of time by yourself. You always struck me as a party kind of guy."

"Are we meeting Alden?" Chal grabbed his wallet, and gestured for Percy to precede him from the apartment.

"Yes. We found a wonderful little restaurant a couple of blocks from the pub. I know the address. Alden will get us a table." Percy slipped his arm through Chal's while they wandered down to the lift. "You don't have anything to say to my comment?"

"What comment? The one where I was a party guy?"

"Yes." Percy hit the sled call button, found on the street lamps.

While they stood on the sidewalk, waiting for the sled, people stared at them. Chal was pretty sure they weren't looking at him. As a Tramp, he was tall, broad and very plain. His brown hair and eyes weren't anything special. No, the people walking past them were looking at Percy, whose blond hair and lavender eyes marked him as a Gypsy. The exotic Gypsies and the elusive Thieves fascinated normal Beasors, but Tramps didn't draw the same kind of attention.

Chal accepted the fact that he would never garner the looks of awe Percy did, and he didn't mind it. In many ways, he liked people not having any expectations of him—it made it easier for him to do his job.

Of course, Tramps weren't used for the exciting or fun jobs. They were mostly transportation specialists. Being able to flash between universes made it easy to grab items other Beasors wanted. He often made runs to Pillian, picking up crates of wine for Alden, because Percy's favourite wine was Pillian, and Alden would pay any price to make Percy happy. Yet there were times when he was asked to take more valuable things, and he'd taken a job or two like that. They were usually more lucrative than regular transportation gigs.

Their sled arrived and Chal gestured for Percy to climb in first. Once the Gypsy was settled, Chal slid in next to him. Percy typed in their destination and they leant back to enjoy the ride. Chal's phone buzzed, and he tugged it out of his pocket to check the number—it was one of the men who usually recommended him for jobs. He sent it to voicemail, not interested in talking about a new job after how long it had taken to finish the last one. He wanted a few days to relax before he jumped into more work. Stuffing his phone back in his pocket, he sighed. Who was he kidding? After dinner, he would be calling Isaac back and setting up a new client. Percy chuckled, and Chal glanced over at him.

"What?"

"You just can't let work go for a while, can you? You always have to be busy. I should have realised that, and that's where you are most of the time. You're not out partying or fucking every cute thing you can find."

Chal shrugged. "Yeah. I haven't been doing that for a while now. Got old real quick."

"Why do you let people think you're a stud?" Percy frowned when Chal glared at him. "Okay. Well, you're still a stud, but why do you make everyone think you're all about the sex and shit?"

Chal shifted on his seat, not really wanting to talk about his reasons with Percy, but he had the feeling Percy wouldn't let it go until he said something.

"I guess, by acting that way, it's easy to get people to underestimate me. People make stupid mistakes when they think they're smarter than you."

Percy nodded. "I've seen that."

"You have reached your destination." A computerised voice came over the speakers.

The sled stopped and the door lifted. Chal stepped out onto the kerb first before turning and offering his hand to Percy. The Gypsy climbed out and they stood for a moment, looking around.

"Hey."

Turning, Chal watched while Steril and Alden walked up to them. Alden wrapped Percy in a quick hug, brushing a kiss over Percy's cheek. Chal embraced Steril and kissed the Thief on the top of his head.

"It's good to see you again, Steril."

Steril grinned up at him, his bright gold eyes gleaming with happiness. "You're gone a lot, aren't you?"

"No rest for the wicked," Chal joked.

They followed Alden and Percy into the restaurant. The hostess greeted them like old friends and Chal guessed they probably came there often. They were escorted to a private table back in the corner of the room. Chal pulled out a chair for Steril, and the smaller man smiled while he sat. Chal took a seat next to him and they looked over the menu.

After eating, they sat around the table, laughing and teasing. As Chal studied the faces of the men with him, he realised he considered them true friends. He'd spent so much of his life alone, avoiding any relationships or entanglements because he didn't want to risk getting attached. Getting attached to someone hurt when that person decided Chal wasn't enough for him. Not good-looking enough, or ambitious enough, to make his lover happy.

Yet there he was, sitting with three men who thought of Chal as their friend. They didn't expect anything from him except to be their friend in return. He knew he could be that. Hell, he'd already done it for Alden, and got Percy back for him.

When Chal wasn't working, he hung out at Alden's pub, drinking and talking with them. Somehow, without his meaning to, he'd got friends, and he wasn't that upset about it.

Steril glancing at his watch broke Chal out of his introspection.

"I have to get back to the Facility. Lately, it's like I'm on lockdown. If I'm not back by a certain time, the teachers come looking for me. You'd swear I was going to run away or something."

They paid their bills and escorted Steril out to the sled stop. When the right sled arrived, they said goodbye. Alden and Percy flagged down another sled to take them back to the pub.

"Are we going to see you later?" Alden asked after giving Chal a hug.

"Not sure. I have to call my boss back. He might have another job for me, and, if he does, I'll be taking it."

"Why? You just got back from the last one. Do you need money that badly? We could lend you some." Percy rested his hand on Chal's arm.

Chal laughed and shook his head. "No, I don't need any money, but thank you for offering. I like working, Percy, and I don't like sitting around my apartment doing nothing. I can't spend all my off time at the pub. That starts looking desperate and sad."

Alden nodded while taking Percy's hand. "I get it. Well, I hope you'll let us know either way. If it's not a job, stop by for a drink tonight."

"All right. I'll talk to you later."

He got his own sled and headed home. After getting back and changing into some comfortable clothes, he grabbed his phone, dropped on the couch, then dialled the Head Councilman for the Tramps.

"How nice of you to call me back, Chal." The Councilman answered after the phone rang several times.

Chal rolled his eyes, hating how the Tramp always tried to act superior to everyone else. Especially when everyone knew the man had got his position because of political clout, and not because of how powerful his magic was.

"Sorry. I was busy with other things. I got back to you as soon as I could. What do you want?" Chal stretched out on the couch, staring up at the ceiling while waiting for the Councilman to talk.

"I've got a job for you. The client wants to meet you tomorrow at ten to discuss it."

"I just finished two weeks of flashing from one universe to another, almost non-stop. Don't you think

I'd like a little downtime to recuperate?" Chal wanted to roll his eyes at himself.

"Chal, you're one of the strongest Tramps I've ever seen. You, more than any other, don't need time to rest. The client is willing to pay a lot of money for your time, and he specifically asked for you. Seems you have a reputation of retrieving lost things."

He grunted and mentally dismissed what the Councilman had said. Having any kind of reputation meant nothing to Chal. All he wanted was to make money, live a good life, and have fun from time to time.

"Just meet with him, Chal. I'm sure the money he's offering will outweigh your need for a vacation. Remember, you keep sixty per cent of the fee." The Councilman sounded disgruntled about that.

Chal snorted. "I know, and there's a reason why I negotiated that percentage when I agreed to join the union. I'm not doing all the work and letting you get all the money."

Silence greeted his statement, and Chal grinned. Yet, as much as he liked messing with the Councilman and any other of the Tramps in the union, he also knew he'd be taking the job, simply because he hated sitting in his apartment alone. Spending all his free time at the pub wasn't practical, or even safe. Not if he liked being healthy and not a drunk.

"Send me the meeting place, and I'll be there with bells on."

"Don't blow this client off, Chal. He's very rich and connected."

Meaning he'd promised the Councilman support during his next election bid. Chal didn't really care, since he wasn't interested in politics in any capacity.

"I won't. Just get me the right information, and I'll go. I'm not promising I'll take the job, but at least I'll listen to him. I have to go now."

He hung up and dropped his phone to the floor. Closing his eyes, Chal took a deep breath and started to meditate. He needed to rebuild his power stores. While Tramps weren't completely wiped out from flashing, he still did use his power, and it had to be renewed or it would run out.

Chal must have dozed off, because, when his phone buzzed, he jolted awake. His heart pounded while he searched the floor for his phone. The buzzing had stopped by the time he'd grabbed it. The video mail chimed, and he punched in his password to get it.

Alden's face popped up. "Hey, if you're not busy, stop by tonight. I'll give you a free drink. Hell, for what you did to find Percy, I should give you all your drinks for free. See you later."

He deleted the message and pushed to his feet. Going to the pub didn't sound like fun tonight. Chal decided he'd stay in and read. He hadn't done that in a long time, and something told him he shouldn't be around other people at the moment. After grabbing his e-reader, he curled up on the couch with a bottle of his favourite ale and started to read. He had a lot of print books as well, because sometimes he liked holding an actual book in his hand, but tonight he wanted the ease of his e-books.

Later that night, after Chal went to sleep, he dreamt a familiar dream of a man who looked like a Thief, but felt far more innocent than Thieves usually were. Being able to steal anything, even a person's soul, tended to make Thieves jaded and arrogant.

Chal knew it wasn't Steril he was dreaming about, since nothing about the Thief in his dream was familiar. This particular man seemed scared and worried about something. His golden gaze implored Chal to help him, but Chal didn't know what the problem was, and he didn't know if he wanted to get involved, even though it was just a dream and it wouldn't affect his life. God, how terrible a person was he, when he wouldn't even think about helping some stranger in his dream. It wasn't like what he did in his fantasy would spread over to reality.

The stranger reached up and touched Chal's face gently, trailing his fingers over the curve of Chal's chin. *"Will you help me?"*

Staring into those golden eyes, Chal couldn't deny the man. *"I'll do whatever I can,"* he promised.

"I can't let him get a hold of me."

The desperation in the Thief's voice tugged at Chal's heart, and he found himself wanting to do anything to keep this man safe.

"I won't let that happen. You have to trust me."

"I do. I don't know you or even if you're real, but I trust you."

Why did knowing some imaginary man trusted him make him puff his chest out in pride? He rolled his eyes at how he reacted. Of course, it was just a dream, so it really didn't matter how he acted or what he did. He slid his hand around the back of the man's head, burying his fingers in the long, black hair at his nape. The Thief tilted his head up so Chal could bring their lips together in a hard, demanding kiss.

He didn't know how far his dream would have gone because loud noises jerked him from his sleep, and he sat up in his bed, rubbing his eyes. Chal stared up at the ceiling. His neighbour in the apartment above him must have been moving things around. Usually Chal didn't care because he either wasn't around during this time of the night, or he was so deeply asleep he never heard it. It was only when his neighbour had asked him if the noise had kept him awake that he'd found out about his habit of moving furniture.

Chal climbed out of bed and stalked to the bathroom. He glared at his erection when it made it difficult for him to take a piss. Maybe he should jerk off and get the haunting kiss out of his head. It wasn't like he'd ever see the Thief in real life, and nothing led him to believe the man even existed.

It didn't matter how exciting the kiss was in his dream. It wasn't real, and he wasn't going to masturbate to a fantasy. He never had and never would. Hell, it had been easier to find a warm body to rub off on than to imagine the kind of man he actually wanted to sleep with.

His hard-on softened, and he took care of business. After washing up, he went back to bed. He pulled the blankets up around his shoulders, and wiggled to find the most comfortable spot on the mattress. With a sigh, he closed his eyes and allowed sleep to take him again.

* * * *

Palmer opened his eyes and stared up at the water-stained ceiling above him. He pressed his fingers against his tingling lips. Who was the Tramp he had dreamt about? Was he real? Sighing, Palmer shook his head as he climbed out of his bed.

He paced over to the window of his run-down motel room. He didn't really have any idea where he was. He'd been lucky to find a Tramp who would take him to the Earth universe for the small amount of credits Palmer had. Of course, having been kept prisoner most of his life, he didn't have any skills to make a living with—unless he stole people's identities, and he didn't like doing that.

Palmer had found a job washing dishes at a local diner, and his boss paid him enough to afford the crappy room, but Palmer wanted to go back to Beasor. He didn't want to spend his life in this universe. He hadn't slept well since arriving on Earth, but this had been the first night he'd dreamt of anyone. To be kissed like that, even by a dream man, was amazing, and Palmer didn't know how to handle the lingering sensation.

He returned to his bed and didn't even try to go back to sleep. He pulled out a book and opened it. Maybe reading would take his mind off his dreams. Palmer had given up believing in them coming true.

Chapter Two

Chal arrived at the restaurant five minutes before his meeting was due to start and looked around the room. He studied all the customers, making note of where the different exits were. He could never be sure what type of person asked for his services, so it paid to know how to get out if he got uncomfortable.

"Mr Farnsmith?" The hostess approached him.

"Yes?"

"Your companion is already seated. May I show you to your table?" She gestured into the room.

Chal nodded, and followed her when she strolled around the tables towards one in the back. When they approached, a short, balding man stood and held out his hand.

"Mr Chal Farnsmith, I'm glad you were willing to agree to this meeting."

"I agreed to hear what you had to say. I didn't necessarily agree to do what you wanted." Chal shook the man's hand and sat.

The client sat as well. "I'm Hamish Coldston. I need you to find someone for me."

Chal studied Coldston, noticing his small, beady eyes and the way Coldston never met Chal's gaze for longer than a few seconds at a time. Also, he wasn't getting a good vibe from the man. Alden and Percy would probably laugh if he told them, but he chose a lot of his jobs by instinct. Everything about Coldston caused Chal's nerves to scream danger, but he'd promised he'd listen.

"Why do you want this person?" Chal glanced up when the waiter stopped by the table. He gave his order and waited for Coldston to place his before motioning for the Beasor to tell him.

"Palmer stole something from me, and I want you to bring him back. I want my property, and I want Palmer to be punished for stealing from me." Coldston's eyes grew hard.

Chal took a sip of his coffee, not willing to agree to anything before finding out more information. "What did Palmer take from you?"

Frowning, Coldston didn't seem inclined to tell Chal what the object was. "It's something very personal and precious to me. Palmer's a Thief, and he took advantage of my trusting nature to get close enough to steal my treasure."

Trusting nature? Chal gave a mental snort. He had the feeling Coldston was about as trusting as a snake. "Why not talk to the Thief Head Councilman? He should be able to get this Palmer back without you having to pay me my fee."

"I don't want to bring the Council into this. All right, I'll be honest. I don't really want Palmer punished by the Council for what he did." Coldston glanced around like he was making sure no one was close enough to overhear what he had to say. "Palmer made a pass at me, and, when I turned him down, he got mad. I'll admit I've spoilt him, and he's young, so he tends to act out and not think about his actions."

Chal bit his lip to keep from laughing in Coldston's face. Now, Chal knew he wasn't anything special to look at, but somehow he had a hard time seeing a Thief hitting on Coldston. Being a Thief, Palmer would have black hair and gold eyes, much like Steril, and he would more than likely be gorgeous. Maybe it was shallow of Chal to think no one would find Coldston attractive.

"Where do you think Palmer went?"

"I think he's on Earth somewhere. I had someone track him and I'll give you the town where I believe he ended up." Coldston reached down to grab the briefcase at his feet. "I have a folder of information for you."

Chal held up his hand. "I didn't say I'd take the job yet. Why don't I go get whatever he took from you, instead of bringing Palmer back? That's going to be difficult if he doesn't want to come."

"You're the best Tramp in Beasor. I'm sure you'll be able to find a way to get him back here. I don't appreciate him stealing from me. I keep what is mine, and he has no right to leave me."

Something about Coldston's statement didn't sit right with Chal. The gleam in Coldston's eyes when he spoke of keeping what was his made Chal uneasy.

"While I don't want to get the Council involved in Palmer's punishment, I do want him back here. He's very innocent, and hasn't spent much time out in the world. I'm afraid he might not be able to survive without someone looking out for him."

Nothing the man said sounded sincere, but Chal had dealt with clients like that before. He simply made sure they paid him well for overlooking his doubts. Of course, even if Chal wanted to say no to Coldston, he had the feeling the Head Councilman was going to force him to take the job.

"Before I agree to take this job, we have to talk about my fee. I won't do this retrieval for cheap. It's going to cost you a lot," he informed Coldston.

Coldston waved his hand in a dismissive gesture. "I don't care about the cost. I'll pay whatever you ask to know Palmer and my treasure are safe."

What the hell kind of treasure had Palmer stolen? Chal was becoming interested in spite of his misgivings. He thought about the fee he'd charged his last client, and tripled it. He didn't feel bad about upping his fee by so much, because Coldston's attitude rubbed him the wrong way.

The man acted like Chal was there to serve him, and wasn't interested in telling Chal the entire truth about why he wanted Palmer back. Oh yeah, Chal believed there was more to the story than Palmer taking something important from Coldston. If it were that simple, Coldston would have just gone to the Council and asked for them to go after Palmer.

Yet Chal doubted Coldston wanted the Council messing in his business, so he probably could have asked for more credits, and Coldston would have paid. Chal didn't want to get too greedy, though.

"All right." He wrote down his fee on a napkin, and shoved it across the table towards Coldston. "Here's my fee."

Coldston looked at the number and his jaw tightened. He glared at Chal, who shrugged.

"Something tells me this job's going to be a lot more difficult than first described. So the price goes up. If you don't like it, go to the Council and have them send someone after your Thief." As intrigued as Chal was by the job, he didn't need it, and didn't care if Coldston went with someone else.

"No. I'll pay the fee. Send me your account number, and I'll transfer half. You'll get the rest when you return Palmer to me." Coldston motioned for the waiter to bring the cheque.

"I'm sorry. Who told you I'm willing to split my fee? I don't do that." Chal didn't even think about reaching for the bill. Coldston wanted the meeting, so he could pay for the food.

"Your Councilman said it wouldn't be a problem." Coldston frowned.

"I'm sure he did." He drew the napkin back to him, and wrote down a different number. He shoved it back to Coldston. "Here. This is my percentage of the fee. You send this to me, and you can withhold the Council's portion."

Coldston's eyebrows shot up when he saw the amount Chal asked for. "Your cut seems pretty high for Tramp work, even if you are the best."

"Yeah well, you want the best, you have to pay for it. I don't care whether you hire me or not." After standing, Chal pulled out his business card. He tossed it on the table. "Call me if you decide to go ahead with this, and I'll give you the account number."

He turned, then strolled out of the restaurant. Coldston would be calling him before the day was over, but the man would not be happy about it. Chal wasn't going to take only half at the beginning. He hated that practice, seeing it as a way to cheat him out of the rest at the end by saying he hadn't completed the task.

While strolling down the sidewalk, he thought about the job. What was the treasure Coldston wanted so badly he'd hire a Tramp to hunt down the Thief? Chal liked flashing to the Earth universe. He enjoyed hanging out with most humans, though he understood some of them were messed up, like the bastards who'd held Percy captive.

He didn't spend a lot of time on Earth, because it was far behind Beasor in its technology and attitude. He could kiss a man on the sidewalk in Beasor without anyone saying anything or trying to hurt him. Chal never understood why humans hated people who were different from them. It didn't make any sense, but Chal had learnt to accept the rituals and habits of the worlds he visited whilst flashing between the universes.

Chal stopped to stare in a window, studying the items. He wasn't interested in them, but he was interested in the man who had been following him since the restaurant. Chal caught the man's image reflected in the glass, and grunted.

Swinging around to face him, Chal glared. "What the hell are you following me for, Weston?"

Chal's former boyfriend held his hands up in the air and grinned. "What makes you think I was following you? This is a public sidewalk. I could have just been taking a walk."

"Bullshit. I saw you standing across the street when I entered the restaurant, and for some reason, you were still there when I left it. The minute I was far enough away, you crossed the street and started following me."

"I think you're being paranoid, love." Weston reached out and trailed his fingers over Chal's cheek. "I've missed you."

Chal stepped away from Weston's touch. He fought the need to scrub his skin where Weston's fingers had rested.

"Don't act like you haven't missed me, Chal. I know you haven't been with anyone since we broke up. Did you care about me that much?" Weston smirked.

"How do you know I haven't been with anyone? Have you been following me?" Chal stiffened, realising he wouldn't put it past his former lover to keep track of his whereabouts.

Weston shrugged. "I thought I'd wait until you cooled off a little before approaching you again. I still don't know why you're so upset with me."

"You dumped me because I wouldn't steal priceless artefacts from an Earth museum. I won't do that. I'm not a Thief — of any kind." He glared at Weston.

"Ah, come on, honey. It wouldn't have mattered. They wouldn't have noticed them missing, and we would have been rich. I know a ton of people who wouldn't have asked how we got those artefacts." Weston grinned. "I would've split the finder's fee with you."

Chal gritted his teeth, knowing hitting Weston wouldn't solve the problem, though it would make him feel better. While he was deciding exactly what to do, someone called his name. Weston's mouth dropped open, and Chal smiled when the person yelled his name again, and he recognised who it was.

After turning, he held his arms open to give Percy a hug. The Gypsy stepped close, and hugged him tight before brushing a quick kiss over Chal's lips. He was a little shocked Percy would do that, but it seemed his friend might have an idea who Weston was.

"I'm so sorry I'm late. I was hoping to be here when you finished with your meeting, but you know how long it takes me to get ready in the morning." Percy winked at Chal before facing Weston. "I can't help it. We didn't have time to play this morning, and I just get so turned on when I think of Chal. I had to take care of my urges before I could leave our bed."

Chal coughed to cover his laughter. He hoped Alden would have a sense of humour about this when Percy told him. Weston looked stunned, not only by Percy's words, but by the Gypsy's appearance as well.

"I'm Percy. Who are you?" Percy held his hand out, practically forcing Weston to shake it.

"I'm Weston, an old friend of Chal's."

"Really? He's never mentioned you to me. Hmm…well, it could be because we don't talk a lot when we're alone. There are other things I'd rather be doing with Chal than talking." Percy glanced down at his watch. "Oh, we better get going. We have to meet with the movers."

Chal simply nodded at Weston—he had nothing left to say to the bastard. He wasn't interested in getting back together with him, knowing Weston only wanted him for his power. He offered his arm to Percy, who rested his hand in the crook of Chal's elbow.

They wandered off, doing their best to look like a couple very much in love with each other. When they reached the corner, Chal quickly glanced over his shoulder and sighed.

"Weston's gone," he told Percy.

The Gypsy didn't remove his hand from Chal's arm. He reached out to push the button, calling a sled to their location. Chal kept his mouth shut, knowing

Percy would start asking questions when he felt like it. As much as Chal didn't want to talk about Weston, he knew he owed Percy some kind of explanation.

"Wait until we get back to my place. I'm sure Alden would like to hear this as well, especially if anyone saw my little performance." Percy gestured to the sled as it pulled up to the kerb.

"I owe you a drink or two for helping me out with Weston." He allowed Percy to slide in first before he joined him.

"Who is Weston? You didn't look happy with him." Percy settled against the seat and turned to look at him.

Chal swiped his credit card, and punched in the address of Alden's pub. He leant back and folded his arms over his chest before sighing.

"Weston was a mistake, and I wish you'd never met him."

Percy patted Chal's knee sympathetically. "I have men in my past I wished I'd never slept with. I try not to think about them anymore. I have Alden now, and I'm forgetting what I did before I chose him."

Chal laughed. "You might be able to forget, but I guarantee Alden still remembers the men you brought back to the apartment."

"I hope not. I was a bit of a man-whore for a while there." Percy grunted when Chal shot him a sceptical glance. "All right. For most of the time, until I got my head out of my ass and figured out Alden was the best man I'd ever met."

"Well, you are lucky to have Alden. If I hadn't seen—in the first seconds of meeting him—how in love with you he was, I would have made a play for him," Chal admitted.

Percy's smile held understanding and total agreement. "I wouldn't doubt that, but as I've figured out, Alden wouldn't have looked at anyone else. That's one of the things I love about him. I can trust him."

"Must be nice to be able to trust your boyfriend," he muttered.

"Alden's one of a kind," Percy agreed.

They fell into a comfortable silence as they continued across town. Chal tried to think of any of his work associates he felt friendly enough with to not fill the air with words. He admitted to himself that Percy, Alden, and Steril were his only true friends.

What a sad commentary on his life that it was only in the last year he'd loosened his usual paranoia. Chal considered those three men his closest friends. He'd do anything for them, even rescue one of them from demented assholes.

The sled slowed to a stop, and Chal watched the door lift open. After climbing out, he helped Percy—the Gypsy emerged from the sled like a king leaving his carriage. Percy's arrogance was understandable. Gypsies were the most beautiful of Beasors, with their blond hair and lavender eyes. They exuded sex like a pheromone or something, inspiring lust in anyone who saw them. Chal felt it in his groin each time he saw Percy after being away from him for a while. Yet after spending time with Percy he'd forget about wanting to fuck the Gypsy, and he'd see the love Percy had for Alden.

Four types of Beasor populated their home planet. Gypsies, like Percy, were beautiful, sexual and in touch with nature and animals. Thieves, like Steril, were almost as beautiful as Gypsies, but with the ability to steal anything, even souls.

Then there was Chal, a Tramp, who was a transportation specialist because he could flash between universes without losing any power. Yet he was ordinary-looking, brown hair and eyes. Nothing to make anyone who didn't know about Tramps suspect he had power.

Alden, Percy's lover, was just an ordinary Beasor, no power except the ability to deal with Percy and all of the Gypsy's flightiness. Yet Chal sometimes wished he was like Alden—no special powers—and could simply be a bartender, or something ordinary.

"Percy, where in the hell did you pick up this Tramp?"

They looked up when Alden yelled from the window a floor above the pub. It was early in the day, so Alden wouldn't have been needed downstairs yet.

"I saved him from an old mistake, then I convinced him to come and have lunch with us." Percy smiled up at Alden, and even Chal could tell Alden was the love of Percy's life.

"Well then, bring him up, love. I want to hear about this old mistake." Alden winked at Chal who blushed. "Something tells me it'll make Chal squirm."

"You're a sadistic bastard," Chal yelled before he allowed Percy to drag him into the alley where a metal staircase led up to his apartment.

Alden opened the door when they reached the landing, and Percy fell into his arms. Chal managed to squeeze past them into the entryway as they kissed. After kicking off his shoes, he wandered into the living room and flopped onto the couch. He tried not to listen to the sounds coming from the other room, but it was getting harder to ignore them.

He snorted. Harder was the right word. His cock pressed against the front of his pants, and piling lust on top of the annoyance he'd felt seeing Weston again didn't make him happy.

"Could you two go in the bedroom or just stop making out? It's not very nice to rub your happiness in a friend's face," he pointed out, loudly enough for them to hear him.

He heard Percy giggle, and he stayed facing forward when the Gypsy strolled in, joining him on the couch. He scowled when Percy leaned his head on his shoulder.

"Is someone a little frustrated?" Percy teased. "You do know you can have just about any man, on any given night, at the pub?"

"I do know that, but it's not fun anymore." Chal rubbed his hand over his face. "God, I must be getting old or something. Sex for sex's sake isn't nearly as exciting as it used to be. Don't get me wrong—I'm not going to become celibate or anything like that, but I'd like a guy to stick around and have breakfast with me the next morning."

"Do you tell them that, or do you just assume they know you wouldn't mind them staying?" Percy settled back against the cushions and studied him. "Most of the time, it's given that, if you pick a guy up at a bar, you don't want the awkward morning-after moments."

Chal braced his elbows on his knees and stared at the floor. "I know that. Since I first started having sex, I've kicked a lot of men out of my bed right after we've come. At least I made sure they enjoyed themselves before I shoved them out the door."

Percy hummed softly. "I'm not sure admitting you've been a slut is a good thing, honey."

He rolled his eyes at Percy's comment. "If I was at a bar, there would be a lot of guys who'd like to hear that I'm easy. What do you care? It's not like I'm trying to hit on you or even pick you up. I know you're not interested in sleeping with me."

"He better not be," Alden shouted from the kitchen.

"Not anymore. At one time, I considered it, but I'm a one-Beasor guy now." Percy raised his voice to answer Alden, and a grunt came from the other room.

"Thanks for that." Chal nudged Percy with his elbow.

Percy smiled. "Anytime, Chal. Let's back to what you were telling me. You're looking for a more serious relationship?"

Chal nodded.

"But I thought Weston was an ex-boyfriend? He seemed rather interested in getting back together with you." Percy curled his legs up underneath him, and propped his chin on the back of the couch. His lavender gaze almost seemed to bore into Chal, plunging into the deepest, darkest places in his soul.

Chal shifted, uncomfortable with the way Percy stared at him. "I wouldn't go back to Weston, even if he were the last man on Beasor. We dated for six months, and I totally believed he was the right one for me. I was an idiot."

"Why?" Alden asked as he walked in from the kitchen.

"Because he asked me to steal artefacts from an Earth museum. I told him to hire a Thief, since they don't care what they take. He believed that, because I'd said I loved him, I wouldn't have a problem taking them."

Alden nudged Percy, and sat beside the Gypsy, wrapping his arm around Percy's shoulders. "I hate the fact my fellow Beasors don't have a problem using you magical ones for their own advancement. Whatever happened to getting ahead on your own?"

Grimacing, Chal didn't glance up at his friends. "I've gotten used to being used like that, but mostly for transportation or retrieval. I'd never knowingly steal from anyone. That's why I do my research before I accept a case. I should've done as thorough a job vetting Weston as I do my clients."

"Honey, letting yourself fall in love isn't a bad thing, even if you do end up hurt. We all need to learn what we truly want in a partner, and each broken relationship is a learning experience." Percy patted his arm again.

"Right. So you kicked Weston to the kerb, and haven't talked to him until today. What'd he want with you?" Alden brought the conversation back to Weston, someone Chal didn't really want to discuss.

"He thought I'd be interested in getting back together with him. I guess he's been following me around, or at least keeping an eye on me. He knew I haven't been with anyone since we broke up." Chal held up a hand to keep Percy from talking. "With anyone seriously. Not that it would have mattered to Weston. He takes what he wants, and doesn't give a shit if anyone's hurt by it or not."

"We've all met people like that," Alden sympathised. "Lunch is ready, if you're hungry."

After standing, he followed Alden and Percy into the kitchen. "I actually already ate, but go ahead. I'll have a drink, though."

Alden gestured towards the refrigerator. "Drinks are in there. Grab whatever you'd like."

He grabbed a bottle of ale before joining the pair at the table. After having seen his ex, watching Alden and Percy together drove home how lonely he really was. God, maybe he should go out that night and find an anonymous fuck. Maybe that would help rid him of the strange lassitude he'd been feeling lately.

"What are you going to do about all of this? You met with a new client today, right?" Alden asked after a few minutes of silence, in which he and Percy had taken a bite or two of their lunch.

"I'll go home, and do a deeper background check on the guy who wants to hire me. See if there's anything I should be worried about." He stopped, remembering how uneasy he'd felt when Coldston had explained what his mission would be.

Percy eyed him. "What's wrong now?"

Chal shook himself. No point in telling his friends about his misgivings. While he didn't need the money, he didn't have a reason to stick around Catalai. He'd end up at the pub, drinking Alden's ale and feeling sorry for himself.

"Nothing's wrong." He swallowed the last drop of ale in his bottle, and stood. "I'm heading home to do my research. I expect my client will call tomorrow when he realises he can't change my percentage of the price. I want to be ready to leave as soon as he calls."

"Let us know when you go, so we don't freak out too much if we don't hear from you for a while."

"Will do."

Chal hugged Percy and Alden, leaving his friends to finish their meal without a third wheel intruding. When he got down to the street, he called for a sled, and planned how he was going to start his digging into Coldston's past.

Chapter Three

Chal's phone rang, causing him to stretch and stand. He glanced over at the clock while he strolled across his living room to answer it. He'd gone to bed rather early last night, and had got up at a decent hour to continue his information gathering on Coldston.

It looked like he'd lost track of time, since it was about four hours since he'd started. The ringing of the phone seemed to grow more insistent. He held his hand over it, debating whether he should let it go to voicemail or not. Shaking his head, he picked it up. Chal figured Coldston would be annoyed that he hadn't answered on the first ring.

"What took you so long?" Coldston's question charged through the phone like a boxer on attack.

Chal held it away from his ear and took a deep breath before answering, "Hello, Mr Coldston. How are you this morning?"

He could almost hear Coldston grind his teeth in irritation. Chal didn't care what the man thought of him as long as he paid him.

"I need the numbers to the account you want your payment transferred into."

"Guess you couldn't get Isaac to budge on the price for the job, huh? It wouldn't have mattered if you had. It doesn't come out of my share."

He knew it bothered his boss that nothing could be done about Chal's percentage. Chal had negotiated it with the last Tramp Head Councilman, and, once it had been signed, neither party could renegotiate it.

After giving Coldston the numbers, Chal said, "I'll start on the job as soon as I get confirmation all of the money has been received."

"You don't trust me." It definitely wasn't a question.

Chal snorted. "Coldston, I don't trust anyone, especially when it comes to money. I'll be in touch when I've made contact with your Thief."

He hung up before Coldston could say anything else. He wasn't interested in talking to the man anymore. Chal simply wanted to get the job over with, though he still wasn't a hundred per cent sure he should even take it. All the information he'd found on Coldston said the man was dangerous, and very rich. He wasn't interested in rules or laws. He did what he wanted, and fuck whoever was in the way. That didn't bode well for Chal making it out of their work arrangement without being screwed, but he was going to do his best not to suffer any damage.

His computer beeped, drawing him back to the couch. With a click of the mouse, he woke up the screen, and typed in the password for his accounts. A smile danced along the edges of Chal's lips—Coldston was trying to hack into Chal's account, but it didn't matter. By the time the man got into the first one, all of his money would have been transferred out.

Chal's paranoia forced him to set up multiple accounts, sending all of his money through several hundred different banks. It did eventually settle into a large one, listed under a shell corporation with no ties whatsoever to Chal. He didn't trust most of his clients not to try to get their money back from him somehow.

Maybe it was the type of clients he worked for. Men and women who wanted the best things at the lowest price possible, which was why they used him to transport their items instead of going through normal business channels.

As soon as the last dollar showed up in his deepest account, Chal emailed Coldston to let him know the payment was received, and he would be starting the job within the day. Several files appeared in his inbox. Chal assumed they were information on the Thief Coldston wanted Chal to find.

The fact that Coldston wanted Palmer brought back to Beasor and turned over into his custody, instead of the Supreme Council, caused a warning bell to ring in Chal's mind. Usually, when Thieves stole something, the person robbed wanted them to be punished by the highest law in the land. Yet Coldston seemed to want to take Palmer's punishment into his own hands.

Chal shouldn't have been overly surprised, since Coldston had struck him as being very controlling and possessive of anything he deemed to be his.

He clicked on the first file, opening it up and settling back to read. He needed to get up to speed on his target before he went to Earth to find Palmer. Why had the Thief gone to Earth? There were more remote universes to hide out in, though Chal doubted distance would have stopped Coldston from hunting Palmer down. It was time to learn who Palmer was. Then tomorrow he'd head out to look for him.

* * * *

A few hours later, Chal grunted as he stared at a picture of Palmer. Even though the younger man looked like every other Thief Chal had come across, there was something in Palmer's eyes that spoke to Chal on a visceral level. The innocence in those golden eyes tugged at Chal, and all he wanted to do was find Palmer and hug him.

He shot to his feet and shook his head. Thinking like that was crazy. Whether Chal trusted Coldston or not, there was a reason why the man wanted Palmer, and Chal couldn't forget that Palmer was a Thief. He could be whatever anyone wished of him. Hell, most Thieves didn't care whom they hurt. Well, except for Steril. That Thief was going to get his heart broken — or even his spirit — if he didn't toughen up.

Chal's stomach made an interesting sound, and he realised he hadn't eaten at all that day. He placed an order at the nearest pizza place before settling back on the couch. He continued to study Palmer's picture. What had the Thief stolen that Coldston wanted him found so badly?

Yet the gut-deep instinct Chal had come to rely on warned him something smelt rotten about the whole job. So Chal would proceed with caution and never let his guard down. He wouldn't put it past Coldston to have him followed, and try to nab Palmer himself, so he wouldn't have to pay the rest of the money to the Tramps' Council.

Should he warn Coldston about following that path? The Council never allowed any client to renege on their part of the job, which usually meant payment. The percentage they received for each job went towards the training schools the different Beasors ran, though only Thieves really needed help with their powers. Actually, Thieves needed to learn the ethics and rules surrounding their magic. The punishment for trying something like reneging on their part of the job was very severe and, if a person survived, they never tried it again.

Chal shook his head. It didn't matter to him if Coldston tried to gyp Isaac and the Council out of their money. He still got paid either way. He'd just have to make sure he didn't get hurt in the process.

Coldston's employees had tracked Palmer to Earth, and even had the city he landed in, but it was a guess where he'd ended up after that. Frowning, Chal grabbed his phone and punched in Coldston's number. He gazed out of the window across the room while he waited for Coldston to answer.

"What do you want? I'm not giving you any more money."

He snorted. "Do most of the people you hire call you demanding more money before they even start the job?"

"What do you want, Tramp?" Coldston's voice was cool and he sounded annoyed.

Chal rolled his eyes, glad he didn't have the video feature activated for this call. "What makes you think I'll be able to find your Thief? Once he was on Earth and in the city, if he's smart, he could've easily taken another person's identity and shit. We'd never find him then."

"Trust me, Mr Farnsmith."

Like that's going to happen, Chal thought.

"Palmer isn't the kind of Thief who would do that."

"But he's the kind of Thief who steals something from you," Chal pointed out.

Silence greeted Chal's comment, and he wondered if Coldston didn't like being contradicted. He waited the man out, knowing Coldston wouldn't stay quiet for long.

"Palmer is quirky, like most Thieves. He has unusual ethics, plus he was angry with me. He took off to punish me, Mr Farnsmith, and, while I do understand his motives, I want my things back, and I expect an apology from him."

"An apology? That's really all you're looking to get from him, huh?"

"Once you turn Palmer over to me, Farnsmith, it's none of your concern what I do with him."

Coldston hung up, and Chal held his phone for a few minutes while he digested what Coldston had told him. No matter how he twisted it, none of it added up. Why would Palmer steal something from Coldston, mostly likely pay someone to flash him to another universe, then basically hide in plain sight? Especially when he had the ability to change his appearance at will. A Thief who had stolen something as valuable as Coldston made the item sound wouldn't. Of course, they wouldn't have gone all the way to Earth to hide either.

None of it made sense, and Chal's head began to pound with all the wondering. He wanted to eat before he called Alden to let him know he was leaving the next morning. It was weird to have to check in with someone. Before he had friends, he'd come and go as he pleased, and no one would panic if they hadn't heard from him in a while.

His biological family had never been close. His mother's first husband stopped by the house long enough to get her pregnant every couple of years, then he'd head off to other universes, and probably other families. Chal's mother never really cared because she was too caught up in her own life. She'd have the baby, then hand it off to the nanny.

As the youngest, Chal had never really felt close to his other siblings, though it might have more to do with the fact that their father wasn't his. He had four older brothers and sisters, but their father had disappeared for good about ten years before Chal was born. He was the result of a one-night stand, and by the time he was old enough to interact with the others they were gone, living their own lives.

He hadn't been interested in learning about them, or even meeting them. Chal knew who they were, and roughly where they lived, but he didn't go looking for them. Only three of them were Tramps, and the other was an ordinary Beasor. Maybe it wasn't the right thing to do to ignore his family, but he figured, if they wanted to get to know him, they knew where he was as well. Learning about each other went both ways, as far as he was concerned.

A knock on the door drew him away from his thoughts, and he got up to answer it. The pizza was hot, its delicious scent wafting through his apartment, causing his stomach to rumble again. He'd eat, then call Alden and make plans to meet them at the pub. No reason why he shouldn't have a drink and a dance before starting the new job.

Palmer would be waiting for him on Earth, and he'd solve the rather odd mystery of a Thief who would steal, but wouldn't use his power to disappear and get away with his theft.

* * * *

Palmer glanced up at the clock on the wall of the diner. Sighing, he finished clearing the table he was working on. Only ten minutes left of his shift, then he could go home, put his feet up and sleep for three days. Well, maybe not three days, since he needed to be back at the diner for the evening shift tomorrow, but he could get at least eight hours' sleep before then.

He hefted the rubber tub up, grunting with the effort. One of the few benefits of bussing tables and washing dishes was the building up of his muscles from all the heavy boxes he'd been lifting. Snorting softly, he shook his head. He wasn't ever going to be muscle-bound.

Shoving open one of the swinging doors leading into the kitchen, he looked around. The cook had several different orders cooking on the grill, while the other cook took care of the fries and sides. They nodded their heads at his appearance, but didn't stop what they were doing. He carted the tray of dirty dishes to the sinks, setting it down with a thud on the stainless steel counter.

"Take it easy, kid. Don't want you throwing your back out or nothing."

Palmer smiled at the tall, red-haired lady peering around the door at him. Betty had befriended him the minute he'd walked into the diner for his first day of work. She'd taken him under her wing, and taught him everything he needed to know about surviving as a busboy.

"Don't worry, Betty. I'm building up some big muscles by lugging these things around," he joked, flexing his biceps.

She shook her head in disbelief, and José, the main cook, snorted.

"You'll need to lift a lot more of those to build up any kind of muscle, kid." José winked at him.

"I know." He started filling the sink with hot water and soap. "I've never been able to put on weight."

"No big deal." Betty patted him on the shoulder when she walked past him. "Not every man is meant to have rock-hard abs or an ass you can bounce a quarter off."

Palmer ducked his head, hating the way his cheeks heated at Betty's suggestive remarks. He didn't know if she realised he was gay or not. He'd never given any hints one way or the other, feeling it wasn't any of their business whom he slept with.

She strolled back out into the main diner room. Palmer had taken care of refilling drinks for her customers while she'd grabbed a quick cigarette out in the alley behind the diner. It wasn't supposed to be one of his jobs, but he didn't mind helping out the waitresses when they needed an extra hand.

"You settling in all right?" José asked after plating up a burger and onion rings.

"Yes." Palmer added some cold water to the sink.

"Not exactly what you're used to, huh?"

He shot a puzzled look over at Juan, the other cook and José's brother. "What do you mean?"

"He means it's obvious you aren't from around here, or from this side of the tracks. Do you understand?" José peered at Palmer.

The confused look on Palmer's face must have alerted José that he really didn't have a clue as to what any of it meant.

José chuckled. "Dude, you really aren't from around here."

"Well, no, I'm not. I just moved here." He started scrubbing one of the plates as he frowned. "What does that have to do with what you're talking about?"

"Juan means you've probably never washed dishes before you got a job working here. I'd also bet you never ate at a greasy spoon diner like this one either." José bumped Palmer's shoulder with his when he walked over to one of the refrigerators to grab some food.

Palmer ducked his head. Was it that obvious he was different? Had he stuck out that much? Darn, if that was true, he might have to leave and hide somewhere else. Just because he hadn't seen anyone watching him didn't mean Coldston wasn't looking for him.

"No. You're right. I've never done anything like this, but I'm doing it all right, aren't I? You'd tell me if I was screwing up?" He stared at José with anxiety dancing along his nerves. He really didn't want to lose this job or move away.

To be honest, Palmer hated the Earth city. He wanted to be back on Beasor where he was familiar with the people and the customs. Damn Coldston for messing everything up for him. He'd miss the people at the diner, but he wouldn't miss anything else about this particular universe.

"Sweetheart, they're just teasing you. Of course we'd let you know. You're a good worker, Palmer. We wouldn't let you get away from us." Betty strolled by, glaring at José and Juan for scaring him.

"Good. I don't want to cause you to have to work harder because I'm not doing my job."

A large group of people entered the main dining room, and Betty rushed out to greet them. Palmer got busy washing the dishes, wanting to have this last load done before he left work. While he was rinsing the last dish, the other busboy-slash-dishwasher showed up, and Palmer knew it was time for him to head out.

"You have any plans for tonight, Palmer?" Juan called out as Palmer hung up his apron.

He shook his head and grinned. "Pretty boring tonight, Juan. I'm doing laundry and grocery shopping."

"How can you stand all that excitement?" Juan teased him from where he stood at the deep fryer.

"I must be an adrenaline junkie or something. I'll see you all tomorrow."

He waved to Betty as he strolled through the main room to the front door. After shrugging into his jacket, he eased out of the diner to stand to one side of the entrance. Palmer looked down the sidewalk in both directions, searching for anything—or anyone—that looked out of place. He'd been doing it since he'd arrived, and so far he hadn't seen anyone, but that didn't mean they weren't out there.

Palmer turned up the collar on his jacket, blocking out the wind as he headed in the direction of his apartment. Even though he was still rather naïve about the worlds around him, Palmer knew it was only a matter of time before Coldston found him. But it would have been easy for Palmer to get away.

As a Thief, all he would've had to do was steal someone else's soul or identity, and he could've continued to live on Beasor. But he wouldn't have been living as himself. Also, stealing like that was the very reason he'd run from Coldston.

Once he'd realised Coldston was using Palmer's power as a Thief to hurt others, Palmer had vowed never to steal again. Palmer didn't understand why anyone would see a Thief's magic as a good one. They didn't transport things like Tramps did, or help things grow like Gypsies. Thieves stole from people without caring or worrying about whom they hurt.

Well, at least the Thieves Palmer knew did. Coldston wanted Palmer to be just like them, but Palmer couldn't. He didn't like thinking of how much damage he could do to a person's life by stealing their identity from them, and things like that. Hell, he could even steal their souls, if he focused hard enough.

Stealing souls was the easiest way to kill someone, because the Thief couldn't return it once he'd taken it. Palmer had done research on Thieves when he'd figured out what kind of Beasor he was. Throughout Beasor history, Thieves had been used as assassins, and Palmer had vowed never to become one of those.

So he'd run, going to the last place Coldston would look for him. Coldston looked down on humans, seeing them as lesser creatures. Coldston was an ordinary Beasor with no powers of his own, yet he still saw himself as far superior to anyone else. The only different thing Palmer saw in Coldston was the fact that the man didn't have a conscience. He was perfectly willing to take what he wanted without regard to others' feelings.

Palmer took a deep breath, trying to clear his mind. He didn't want to think about Coldston or his past. It was time to look forward and make an honest living for himself. He tucked his hands in his pockets and trudged on. Being on his own was difficult, but Palmer was discovering he had a knack for surviving.

When he got to his apartment building, he climbed up the stairs to his floor. He stopped in front of his door, and stared at the warped, fake wood finish. The sight of its faded, distressed appearance bothered him for some reason that night. He unlocked it, and shoved through to get inside.

Keys went into a bowl on the dining table and his jacket went in the closet closest to the door. He moved to the middle of the single room and spun around, slowly taking inventory of everything in his space. Depression hit him because there wasn't much. Maybe a little more than when he'd lived at the motel three months ago, but not much. He shuddered, shaking off the melancholy threatening to overtake him.

There wasn't any point in getting upset about any of it. He'd made his choice the moment he'd run away. Dealing with what he had now might be hard at times, but he was still alive, and his honour was intact. Ultimately, as far as Palmer was concerned, that was the important thing.

After he'd told himself that, he went into the kitchen area, needing to eat since he hadn't while at work. He opened his small refrigerator, scanning the mostly empty shelves for something that looked appetising. Maybe he should have eaten at the diner. At least there he got his meals for free.

Rather discouraged, he slammed the door shut and whirled around. It was time to go grocery shopping. He'd got paid yesterday, so he had money for food. Palmer grabbed everything he'd just dropped, along with a reuseable tote bag. He never bought enough stuff to justify more than one bag at a time.

After locking the door behind him, Palmer returned to the street and headed to the store. If he wasn't so hungry, he would've waited until the next day but, if it could, his stomach would be chewing its way to his spine right now.

Palmer grimaced at the grotesque visual his thought conjured up. If he didn't watch it, he would gross himself out and wouldn't be able to eat, no matter how much his stomach wanted food in it. He continued on to the store and bought everything he'd need for the next week.

As he was turning on to his street after the store, the hair at the nape of his neck stood up, and he got the distinct impression someone was staring at him. Palmer didn't pause, knowing he shouldn't let whoever was watching know he was on to them. Keeping his normal pace was difficult, but he did it until he got inside the building.

He raced up the stairs, almost dropping his groceries in the process. He wanted to get to the window as quickly as possible to see if anyone was standing out on the street. He got into his apartment and slammed the door shut before locking it. Somehow he managed to set the bag on the counter without losing anything.

Palmer got to the window and peered around the curtain, his heart pounding loudly in his ears. There were people wandering up and down the sidewalks, though none of them seemed particularly interested in his building. Snorting softly, Palmer turned away.

What kind of idiot was he? Did he really think that, if there was a person spying on him, they would be wearing a sign or something to make them stand out from the crowd?

He was tired, and his imagination kicked into overdrive. Palmer strolled into his kitchenette to put the items away, deciding what he wanted to eat — something easy and quick because he could feel exhaustion tug at him.

Food prepared, Palmer wandered over to his bed and sat to eat. He glanced around the smallish loft he'd rented. The tiny kitchen area flowed into the combined living and sleeping area. The only separate room was the bathroom, and thank God for that. He finished his meal while he remembered what his room at Coldston's mansion had looked like.

Sure, it had been bigger than his current apartment. Hell, the bathroom had been bigger than the space Palmer sat in now. But all the spaciousness and luxury hadn't hidden the bars on the windows and the locks on the doors. Nothing had made up for the fact that his luxurious living space had been a prison, holding him for the whims of a madman.

After returning his plate to the kitchen, Palmer stripped and climbed under the covers. He hadn't turned on any lights when he'd got back from the store. Just another example of letting his paranoia take control of him. If there had been someone watching him they wouldn't have known which apartment was his.

He curled up with a sigh. He hoped his dream man would appear to kiss away his worries again. Palmer didn't want to have a nightmare about Coldston finding him, and dragging him back to Beasor. If that happened, Palmer knew he'd never get free again and, eventually, he'd give in to Coldston's demands.

Chapter Four

Palmer glanced up when the bell over the diner door chimed. He froze, and his mouth dropped open. The rubber tub he held, filled with dishes, threatened to slip out of his hands while he stood in shock.

"Who are you?" he asked, not caring how rude he sounded.

The man narrowed his eyes at Palmer while he studied him. Palmer had been cleaning one of the booths in the back corner where the lighting wasn't very good. He knew his face was mostly in shadows.

"Seems rather a rude way to talk to a customer." The man's deep voice caused shivers to race down Palmer's spine.

Christ! Palmer closed his eyes and heaved a mental sigh. The man had his dream lover's voice. What kind of magic existed to bring his lover from his dreams to life, and have him appear at the diner? He was pretty sure he wasn't sleeping anymore.

"Could I get a cup of coffee?"

The stranger stepped closer to him, and a shudder of fear cut through Palmer when he realised the man was a Tramp.

Damn it. A Tramp appearing at the diner told Palmer Coldston had found him. Palmer got the tub on the table before he dropped it. He clutched his hands together and glanced around, trying to decide how to get away.

"Well, hell," the Tramp said quietly. "Just my luck."

"Who are you? Did Coldston send you?"

"I'm Chal, and yes, Coldston did send me to retrieve what you stole from him."

Palmer shook his head. "I didn't steal anything from that bastard. Well, except maybe myself," he muttered.

Chal frowned, but didn't seem inclined to leave. Yet he didn't look like he was going to grab Palmer and flash him back to Beasor, either. Sweat trickled down Palmer's back, and his hands trembled. He'd kill himself before he went back to Coldston.

He watched Chal scrub his face with his hand, and Chal sighed.

"You and me need to talk. Something has been off about this fucking job since the beginning." Chal looked at Palmer. "When do you get off work?"

"In an hour." Palmer didn't want to talk to Chal. He wanted to run as far away as possible from the horror the Tramp represented.

Yet, even though his survival instincts screamed to run, there was a more subtle voice telling him to trust Chal. There had to be some reason why he'd dreamt of this particular Tramp for the months since he'd run from Coldston.

He shook his head, forcing the voice out of his mind. The only way he'd survive was by trusting no one, because he knew Coldston would do everything in his power to get him back.

"I'll be back to get you in an hour. Don't even think of ducking out of here early. I know where you live."

Palmer stared at Chal. "You were watching my building last night," he accused.

Chal's expression told him all he needed to know. He was so screwed. Once a Tramp took a job, he didn't quit until he got what he was sent after, and Palmer didn't have a chance of escaping. *Unless you steal someone's soul. It would be really easy to do. Coldston made sure you knew how to do it.*

Again the voice in his head tempted him, but Palmer hated this suggestion even more than he did the first one. Trusting Chal would be healthier for his soul in the long run, yet neither option was what Palmer really wanted.

"Palmer, sweetie, are you okay? This guy isn't bothering you, is he?"

Betty came to stand by his side. Hands on her hips, she glared at Chal. Palmer cleared his throat and shot her a tremulous smile.

"No, Betty. He's a friend from where I grew up. We're just making plans to meet up after work."

Palmer didn't want to cause problems for Betty or anyone else he worked with. They'd become good friends over the months he'd been there.

Chal flashed her an innocent grin. "That's right, ma'am. I told Palmer's mother I'd check on him when I got into town. I swear I'm not going to do anything to him."

She didn't look totally convinced. "Just because you're an old friend doesn't mean I'm not keeping an eye on you. Palmer doesn't have to go with you if he doesn't want to."

Palmer opened his mouth to promise he was all right talking to Chal. Before he could get a word out, Chal laid his hand on Palmer's arm. Skin touching skin for the first time in reality created an arc of electricity between them. Palmer gasped as his cock instantly hardened and every atom in his body strained towards Chal. He wanted to tear his arm away, and yet he wanted to press closer, begging for more of Chal's touch and warmth.

Chal blinked, and Palmer could see the Tramp seemed to be reacting in the same way as he was. He guessed it made things a little better, knowing the attraction wasn't just one-sided.

"Betty," Chal said, after checking the nametag on Betty's blouse. "I need to talk to Palmer about some personal things. If it makes you feel better, we'll stay here at the diner and talk after he gets done working. I have no interest in hurting him."

The sincerity in Chal's voice almost convinced Palmer they were old friends getting reacquainted after being apart for a while. He jumped when Chal squeezed his arm in a warning.

"Right. We'll stay right here." Palmer shot a look at the clock. "I have to get back to work, Chal. I'll see you in forty-five minutes or so."

"Great. Nice to meet you, ma'am." Chal bowed slightly in Betty's direction before he strolled out.

"Whew! Honey, if they grow the men like him where you're from, I wouldn't have left." Betty fanned herself with her order pad.

Palmer had to grin at that. "Like your men macho and rugged, huh?"

She winked at him. "Of course. You're beautiful, Palmer, but I want to be the prettiest one in bed."

Mirth caught him off guard, and his laugh burst from him. Betty started laughing with him, and soon they were holding each other up while giggling. After several minutes, they got themselves under control and he snatched up the tub of dirty dishes, taking them back to the kitchen. Betty followed close behind.

"I meant what I said. You don't have to meet with that guy if you don't want to. No matter how good-looking he is." Betty wrapped her arm around Palmer's shoulders. "You didn't look happy to see him when he first walked in."

Palmer dropped his gaze to the sink. He didn't think he could lie while looking into her eyes. "I was just surprised to see him is all. I didn't think anyone would come looking for me after I left."

"Didn't leave on good terms?" Juan asked from where he stood by the grill. It was his turn to run the kitchen, since José had the day off.

"Not really. I had to go because of a difference of opinions, I guess you could call it."

He mentally rolled his eyes. It was a huge difference of opinions, and he shouldn't have been as surprised as he had been when Chal had walked in. Coldston wasn't about to let his golden goose go free.

Betty bumped their hips together, getting his attention. "Tell me the truth. Is he a real friend of yours or just someone from back home come looking for you?"

"All right, so we aren't friends, but I've been dreaming about him since I arrived here three months ago." He blurted his admission out, then his face felt like it caught on fire as he blushed.

"Ah, we're getting somewhere now. Those dreams could be the reason why I thought you were going to jump his bones out there in the dining area."

"It was that obvious?" Groaning, Palmer covered his face with his apron. "God, I hope he didn't notice anything."

Betty chuckled. "Honey, I think he was too busy trying not to kiss you silly to notice how you were reacting to him."

"Really?" Palmer peered at her over the edge of his apron.

"Yes, really." She hugged him, then let him go. "Let's get moving. We have customers out there, and the tables aren't going to clean themselves."

It was getting busier, and Palmer hoped they got swamped with people, so he would be too busy to think about the coming confrontation with Chal. He set the tub of dishes in the sink, knowing the other busboy would be getting the rest of the tables cleaned off and set up.

As he waited for the water to fill the sink, Palmer let his mind wander back to Chal, and a thought struck him. Why hadn't the Tramp simply grabbed him and flashed them both back to Beasor? It wouldn't have done anything to Chal, but it would have wiped Palmer's strength out for a day or two.

Had Chal recognised him from their dreams? But that wouldn't have been possible, unless they'd been having the same ones. Though why would it be impossible? He wouldn't have believed the man of his dreams existed if Chal hadn't walked in. God, the things they'd done in his dreams. If he hadn't been so afraid of him, he'd have been all over the Tramp like bees on nectar.

Palmer reviewed their conversation, or at least what Chal had said. Something about the job being off from the beginning. What had he meant by that? Was that comment the clue as to why Chal hadn't snatched Palmer the moment he'd figured out who he was?

His head began to pound and he tried to force his worries and thoughts to the back of his mind. It wasn't doing him any good to keep analysing Chal's actions. The Tramp would tell him soon enough. Maybe he would give Palmer a chance to explain, or at least give him an opportunity to change his mind about taking Palmer back.

Having never interacted with any Beasors except for Coldston, Palmer didn't know what to expect from the Tramp. Would there be any possibility of understanding from one magical Beasor to another?

Coldston had always told Palmer that, if people found out what he could do, they would try to lock him up and drain him dry. Of course, that was exactly what Coldston had done, and he would've succeeded, but Palmer had grown a steel spine and had escaped.

Once he'd decided to go, it had taken a long time to plan, with careful hoarding of money and things he could use to bribe people. There were hours, days and even weeks, when he hadn't believed he would make it. When he'd accepted that his place in the world was to do Coldston's bidding until he died. Then a little, soft voice in his heart would tell him there was more out in the world than the bars he stared through every night.

Palmer took a deep breath and straightened his shoulders. He would do whatever he had to do to stay free. If, for some reason, Chal took him back to Coldston, Palmer would immediately start plotting his next escape. It would be far more difficult the second time, but he wouldn't resign himself to living as Coldston's prisoner. Never again.

Once the rush started, Palmer didn't have time to think of his upcoming talk with Chal. He had to wash dishes, reset tables and get drinks for customers when Betty and the other waitresses were busy. He lost all track of time until he turned to head back to the kitchen, and Chal stood in his way.

"I can see you're busy. When you can get away, I'll be sitting in that booth." Chal pointed to the booth farthest away from the kitchen and the other people in the diner. "Like I said, please don't make me come and find you. I know which apartment is yours."

Palmer swallowed loudly, and squeaked, "Okay. I'll be right there."

"Thank you."

Chal watched Palmer walk away from him, trying to keep his gaze on the Thief's back and not his ass. It was hard to do when the faded jeans he wore, and the strings of his apron, showed off Palmer's butt quite nicely, framing those pert cheeks. Shaking his head to clear the lust from it, Chal turned to go and sit in the booth.

"I don't know who you are, but something's telling me Palmer and you aren't really friends." Scowling, Betty set a mug of coffee in front of him.

"We didn't know each other very well, but I am here to talk to him about going home. He doesn't belong here." Chal gestured in the vague direction of the kitchen.

Betty propped her fists on her ample hips and glared at him. "Palmer is fitting in just fine. He likes working here, and I don't appreciate the insinuation that there's something wrong with this diner or the people who work here."

He gritted his teeth to keep from snapping at her. Obviously, Palmer had made a good impression on his fellow workers, and Betty was only trying to protect him. Yet Chal just wanted to get this job over with and go back to Beasor, where everything was so much cleaner and brighter.

Earth wasn't as advanced as Beasor, and they still used gasoline to run their machines. The stench of burning fossil fuels stung his nose, causing him to want to scratch it all the time. He swore he looked like a rabbit twitching his nose to get rid of the smell. The star providing light to Earth was weak, so it wasn't nearly as bright during the day as it was on Beasor.

The planet was nice to visit, but Chal didn't want to stay, or even spend any more time than necessary there. He pasted on a smile for Betty, knowing she didn't find him nearly as charming as most people did.

"Nothing against you, your friends, or the diner, but come on, Betty. You and I both know Palmer isn't meant for dishpan hands and aching feet. He's brighter than that. Hell, he shines, and staying hidden in the back of a kitchen isn't the best thing for him."

There was a slight softening in the lines of Betty's face. Chal was getting to her, and he wasn't afraid to push his advantage. He reached out to rest his hand on her arm.

"I'm not here to hurt Palmer, Betty. I want to talk to him. See if he's determined to stay here, or if I can entice him to come back home with me. You can keep an eye on us the entire time we're here. We just need some privacy to talk."

Sighing, she nodded. "All right. I can tell you're sincere about not hurting him but, if he doesn't want to go home, you better not make him. Everyone has a right to live their lives the way they want to, not how others wish they would."

"Yes, ma'am."

"Betty, don't you have customers to look after?" Palmer spoke from behind her.

She looked at the Thief, and smiled. "Yes, I do. I thought your friend might like some coffee. I'll leave you two to talk."

They watched her stroll away, and Palmer laughed softly before he sat across from Chal. Silence reigned between them while Chal doctored his coffee the way he liked. He wasn't sure how to broach the subject he actually wanted to talk about, and it wasn't about taking Palmer back to Beasor.

"How is it possible I've been dreaming of you for the past several months?" Palmer's quietly spoken question echoed Chal's inner thoughts.

"You have?" He stopped stirring his drink to stare at Palmer. "When did they start?"

Palmer shrugged. "Around the time I came here. I thought I was homesick, so I was dreaming of someone who reminded me of Beasor."

"Do you have a boyfriend back home?" Chal wasn't sure why he had asked that question. It wasn't any of his business.

Snorting, Palmer fidgeted with the salt and pepper shakers. "Coldston didn't let me out of his mansion without an escort. There wasn't any way I could meet anyone. Not that I wanted to. All I was interested in was getting away from the bastard."

The bitterness in Palmer's voice nudged some emotion in Chal, but he didn't want to look at it too closely. Had Palmer been dreaming about him for as long as Chal had dreamt about Palmer? None of that really mattered, since it didn't mean Chal would just throw over his job for the Thief. He needed more information before he could make any sort of rational decision.

Of course, his cock thought it would be a great idea to take Palmer back to his apartment and fuck him through the mattress. It wanted to recreate some of those dreams. Thank God Chal wasn't ruled by his dick.

"Okay. We need to talk about why the hell you ran away from Coldston in the first place."

It was time to get down to business. Palmer swallowed, and his gorgeous golden skin paled. Chal fought the urge to reach across the table and cover Palmer's hand with his. This need to protect and befriend Palmer wreaked havoc on him.

"Where do I start?" Palmer shook his head. "I was an idiot and trusted the wrong person."

"It happens to the best of us. Why don't you start at the beginning? We have time, since I didn't let Coldston know I'd found you."

Palmer brought his head up quickly to meet Chal's gaze. "Why didn't you? Coldston'll be furious when he finds out you discovered where I lived and didn't inform him right away."

Chal shrugged. "I don't work that way. I only contact my clients when I'm done doing what they wanted. I don't need anyone looking over my shoulder the entire time I'm working."

"Coldston likes to micro-manage everyone around him. It's one of his many faults." Palmer dropped his gaze again.

"I have an idea what some of his other ones are." He took a sip of the lukewarm coffee and wrinkled his nose in disgust. He shoved the mug away from him. "All right. Tell me about your relationship with

Coldston. I need to figure out why I haven't felt right about this job from the beginning."

Palmer pursed his mouth, and it looked like he was thinking. Chal stared at his plump lips, wondering what they'd feel like pressed against his. After that first inappropriate thought, his mind imagined they were locked in an embrace, naked and straining to come.

His cock stiffened, and Chal shifted in his seat, wanting to reach down and adjust to get more room. Yet he didn't want Palmer to know what he was thinking. It wasn't good policy to let his target know he was attracted to him. Palmer would probably try to use it to talk Chal into letting him go.

"I met Coldston when I was fifteen," Palmer murmured.

"How old are you now?" Chal didn't think Palmer was any older than twenty-one at the most.

"I'm twenty-two." Palmer frowned at the table. "I might be young, but I've lived a lot in my years."

Considering Palmer used to work for Coldston, Chal could just imagine what the Thief had dealt with in the man's employ. He didn't say anything, though. It had to be told at Palmer's pace, and, as far as Chal was concerned, they could take all the time in the world. He'd already got his money, and his payment was non-refundable.

"You've been with Coldston for seven years? What do your parents think of you hanging with the man?"

Sadness painted Palmer's face, and Chal found he didn't like that expression. For some reason, he never wanted Palmer to be sad or upset again. Chal shook his head. He pushed those emotions away because he couldn't afford to get attached to Palmer. Yet he had the sneaky suspicion it was too late, and had been from the moment he'd first dreamt of Palmer.

"I don't know if my parents are alive or not. The last time I saw them was when I was ten. I don't know what happened to them. I came home from school one day, and they were gone. I'm hungry." Palmer jumped to his feet. "I'll be right back."

Chal didn't protest or try to stop him. He watched as the Thief walked into the kitchen. As much as he wanted to chase after Palmer, he stayed in the booth. He tried not to get nervous when Palmer didn't immediately return. The Thief had said he was hungry, so he was probably getting something to eat.

Just as Chal was getting ready to go looking for Palmer, he shoved through the swinging kitchen doors, carrying two plates of food. He set them down on the table before going to get two more cups of coffee.

Obviously the topic of Palmer's parents was painful for him. Chal could understand that since he didn't like talking about his own, yet he needed to learn how Palmer had come to be working for Coldston in the first place. He waited until Palmer had sat and was eating his hamburger, then he continued the questions.

"You've been working with Coldston for seven years? Have you been involved with him in any other way?"

Palmer blinked and blushed. "What does that have to do with what he's accused me of doing?"

"It's more important than you'd think." Chal didn't even glance at the plate in front of him. He wasn't that hungry, and he knew Palmer had used it as an excuse to regroup and collect his thoughts.

"No. We weren't involved sexually, if that's what you want to know." Palmer shuddered, a look of revulsion crossing his face. "I don't think I'd have lasted long if that was part of the job. Thank God, he likes girls."

Chal grunted. All of his research had told him that, but just because a man preferred women didn't mean he wouldn't fuck a man to keep him in line. He wouldn't have put it past Coldston to use any means necessary to keep Palmer under his thumb.

"How did you two meet?" Chal added cream and sugar to his coffee. He didn't really like the stuff, but he would drink buckets of it if it kept Palmer talking.

"I lived on the streets from eleven until I turned fifteen."

Palmer grimaced, and Chal could only guess what the Thief had seen or done to survive for that long. To be honest, though, Chal was surprised a charity shelter or even a well-meaning family hadn't taken in Palmer. Most Beasors didn't believe in abandoning children, no matter what the circumstances. They treasured the young ones, and especially the ones with power.

Hell, the Thieves' Council had even built a facility to help their kind learn ethics, and how to control their power. He thought about Steril, who was the only Thief Chal knew who didn't want to use his power at all. Talk about having strong morals—Steril wouldn't use his powers at all, if he could help it.

"You were never picked up by one of the charities or anything like that?"

"I hid from them. My parents always told me not to talk to strangers. Also, they led me to believe everyone was out to steal me away." Palmer met Chal's gaze. "I never understood why they'd say that then leave me on my own."

As interesting as that sounded, Chal wanted to move on to when Palmer had met Coldston.

"What about Coldston?"

"He caught me stealing something, and he told me he wouldn't call the authorities if I went with him. At that moment, I was more afraid of the police than of Coldston. Looking back, I should have taken my chances with the authorities."

Chal agreed with him. "You're right, but you were fifteen. You took what you thought would be a better deal. Understandable. What went wrong?"

Chapter Five

"I didn't want to do what Coldston wanted me to do." Palmer dropped his gaze to the plate of food in front of him. His stomach roiled, and his mouth went dry. God, he didn't want to talk about any of this.

"What exactly did Coldston want you to do? You said he wasn't interested in you sexually. So what could you do for him then?"

"I'm a Thief. What do you think he wanted me to do?"

"You're right. It was a stupid question," Chal admitted.

Palmer swallowed the snarky comment he wanted to say. Being a smartass wouldn't help his cause.

"Did you do anything he wanted? Did you steal for him?"

"Yes, I did. I'm not proud of what I did, but I have to point out the fact that I didn't know any better. I left school when I was ten, and hadn't even been told about the Facility."

Chal frowned. "Why not? Do you remember whether your parents were Thieves or one of the other magical Beasors? Did they have problems with the training school?"

Palmer had never really dealt with their abandoning him, so he tried to avoid talking about his parents with anyone who asked. Yet, as odd as it sounded, he had the feeling his parents were still alive. They simply didn't want anything else to do with him.

"I've pushed my memories of them to the back of my mind, but I think my father might have been a Thief. I'm not sure about my mother."

Silence filled the booth as he pushed the remaining food around his plate. Chal sipped his coffee, and Palmer wondered what the Tramp was thinking.

Chal reached over and tapped Palmer's hand, getting his attention. "Tell me, what did you steal from Coldston? Why is he so determined to find you and get you back?"

Palmer pulled his hand away from Chal's fingers. He didn't want to think about how his body reacted to Chal's presence. He'd never been so attracted to any man like he was to Chal.

Should he take a chance and tell Chal the whole truth? What did he really have to lose by explaining why he'd run away?

"I stole myself. I'm the treasure Coldston wants back," Palmer confessed.

"You're the possession Coldston hired me to bring back? You don't have any objects you took from him?" Chal shook his head. "I don't understand. He could get another Thief to steal for him."

"He could, but, unfortunately, I know things about his business and his operations. Things he doesn't want the authorities to know."

Chal's expression darkened, causing Palmer to stiffen. What he knew was another topic he didn't want to discuss, but, if he wanted Chal to let him go, he'd have to say something.

"If I tell you, will you let me go?" He gave Chal a hopeful glance.

The Tramp grinned for a second before his expression became serious again. Chal grabbed Palmer's hands and didn't let go when he tried to tug them free. Palmer took a quick look around to make sure no one was paying attention to them, especially Betty. He didn't need her riding in to his rescue.

"Look at me," Chal demanded.

Unless he wanted to cause a scene, there wasn't anything Palmer could do but meet Chal's gaze. The Tramp pinned him in his seat with intense focus.

"I'm not turning you over to Coldston. Not yet, anyway. There's something else going on here and, until I figure out what it is, I'm not giving either of you what you want. I'm not letting you out of my sight, Palmer."

The strength in Chal's voice told Palmer he meant what he said. There wasn't any way Palmer could get rid of the Tramp unless he told Chal everything. Maybe it would ease his nightmares as well.

"He wanted me to steal a man's soul and identity," he whispered, shivering as he remembered the shocked horror he'd felt when Coldston had ordered him to do it.

"You've stolen for him before, not completely sold on the idea it was wrong," Chal pointed out while he let go of Palmer's hands. "What made this different?"

"Hey, sweetie, you two okay?" Betty strolled past, her keen gaze studying Palmer's face.

He nodded. "Yes, but I think we're going back to my place to talk more privately."

She paused to look at them fully. "Are you sure?"

After sliding out of the booth, he gestured for Chal to follow him. "Yes, I'm sure. I'll see you tomorrow, Betty."

He hugged her, and led the way out of the diner. Chal kept silent, just stayed close. Palmer noticed how the Tramp kept his gaze moving, watching everyone around them.

"Are you expecting trouble?" he asked as they headed in the direction of his apartment.

Chal shrugged. "Never know. I wouldn't put it past Coldston to follow me."

"Shit! Do you think he'll send someone to grab me?" Palmer tensed, fear making him even more paranoid.

"I wouldn't put it past him, but probably not right now. He'll wait to see what I'm doing with you." Chal chuckled. "I don't doubt Coldston believes that, if I don't bring you back, he'll get his money back."

"He doesn't?" Palmer had no idea how the actual Councils worked.

He'd never registered with the Thieves' Council. Coldston wouldn't let him, even though it was the law. It was important for all magical Beasors to be registered, so the Head Councilman could control the money being charged by them for jobs. It also helped keep track of the magical Beasors, especially Thieves, who because of their power could steal people blind. There were severe punishments for Thieves caught breaking the law.

"No. My contract says that, even if I don't bring back what my client hired me to get, it doesn't matter. I keep my percentage of the money. I'm not getting screwed by some rich jackass who thinks he's smarter than me."

The bitterness in Chal's voice alerted Palmer, and he grinned.

"Something tells me that's happened before." He turned the corner onto his street.

Nodding, Chal stuffed his hands in his pockets. "It only happened once. After I lost all the money I'd been paid, I swore it would never happen to me again. So I drew up a contract giving me exactly what I wanted."

Palmer wasn't ready to talk about Coldston while outside, so he continued asking Chal about his business. "How did you convince your Council to agree to that?"

"I'm the best Tramp in our universe. I know you're thinking, what's stopping me from taking the money and just not completing my job?"

Palmer nodded. The thought had crossed his mind.

"I'm proud of my record, and I wouldn't do anything to jeopardise it. Not doing my job is the best way to ruin my career. I've never failed at a job once I've taken it, plus I've discovered I'm stronger than most of my fellow Tramps."

He could tell Chal wasn't bragging, but he wasn't totally sure what the Tramp meant by that statement.

"Stronger? What does that mean?"

Chal stopped in front of Palmer's building and watched the people walking by while Palmer unlocked the street-level lobby entrance. Palmer wondered if Chal would answer his question.

"Stronger in that I can flash through more universes without having to rest than my friends. I haven't found my limit, so I can get things others can't, usually faster than other Tramps."

They went inside and Chal walked right behind him up the stairs, almost like he was guarding Palmer's back.

"Why aren't we using the elevator?" Chal motioned to the metal doors.

"It hasn't worked since I moved in. Even if it did, I wouldn't get on it. I don't like small places."

Chal hummed, but didn't say anything. They made it inside Palmer's apartment without anyone jumping out of the shadows at them, and Palmer relaxed slightly. He hung up his jacket while Chal looked around.

"You don't like small spaces, yet you live here." Chal shot him a quick glance.

"It's all I can afford, especially if I want to be free of Coldston. Can't stand out in any way or he'll find me." Palmer dropped onto his couch and stared at the Tramp. "What do we do now?"

Chal joined him on the couch, and Palmer tried to ignore how good he smelt and how nice his warmth felt next to him. He wanted to taste Chal's lips while he was awake. Would they feel different than they did in his dreams?

"We still need to talk, but I can't ignore this anymore."

Chal threaded his fingers through Palmer's hair and pulled him closer. Palmer melted into his touch, needing the kiss as much as he needed to breathe. Savouring the strength in Chal's hands, Palmer pressed their mouths together. The Tramp's lips were firm and gentle as they rubbed against Palmer's. Another tug and Palmer straddled Chal's thighs to bring them even closer.

Palmer gasped when their groins brushed, and Chal took advantage of the sound to sweep his tongue inside. The taste of coffee and cream danced along Palmer's own tongue while he sucked on Chal's. God, it was so much more than their kisses had ever been in his dreams. Of course, this was Palmer's first real kiss, and he was afraid he might come just from the sensation of Chal's lips on his.

Chal slid his hands down to cup Palmer's ass with strong fingers. Palmer moaned at the feel of Chal surrounding him. He wanted them naked in bed together. He wanted to be pinned to the mattress under Chal's body while the Tramp thrust into him hard and fast.

Palmer whimpered when Chal eased them a few inches apart. Blinking, he stared into Chal's dark brown eyes and tried to figure out what he was thinking. It would have been easier if his own mind worked enough for coherent thought.

"Okay, that got a little heavier than I planned," Chal admitted, smiling at Palmer.

"I don't want to stop." Palmer pouted.

He sighed when Chal rubbed his thumb over his bottom lip.

"Neither do I, but we still need to do some talking. After we do that, maybe we can pick up from where we left off."

Chal didn't look happy about stopping, but Palmer guessed he understood why Chal preferred to talk first and fuck later. He slid to the side, but Chal didn't allow him to move any farther away.

"All right." Chal took a deep breath before continuing, "You said Coldston wanted you to steal a man's soul and take his identity. Most Thieves I know don't have a problem with taking a person's identity or simply stealing from people. I do have a friend who has issues with the whole thing. Being at the Training Facility must drive him crazy."

Jealousy surprised Palmer, creeping into his chest while Chal spoke with such affection about his friend. It was silly, since Palmer had no claim to Chal other than a few kisses and some dream sex.

"Do you know what happens when a Thief takes a person's soul?"

Chal shrugged. "Aren't you basically killing them?"

"Yes, and Coldston wanted me to do that to one of his enemies. After I took the man's soul, I was to take his place on the board of some company. Ultimately, Coldston would have bought the company for less than it was worth, because I would have sabotaged the entire business or something like that."

Palmer snuggled closer to Chal, trying to absorb some of his warmth since just thinking of taking some man's soul like that caused him to become chilled.

"Damn. That's serious. Do you have proof that Coldston's done this before? Or were you the only Thief who worked for him?"

"He had a stable of Thieves working for him. I doubt I was the only one he ordered to do it. Yeah, I have proof, but I hid it." Palmer wrung his hands. "I didn't want to let go of my leverage in case Coldston found me. I thought, if I had the information, he'd have to leave me alone."

"It only works if you set up a secondary plan where, if you didn't come back for the information, it would be sent to the right people on Beasor. Where are the files?"

Suspicion raced through Palmer and he sat up, moving away from Chal. He pushed to his feet to pace his apartment. Chal didn't fight him or try to stop him. The Tramp watched with an understanding gaze.

"How do I know you aren't trying to get the files from me before you turn me over to Coldston? Just because we were lovers in our dreams doesn't mean I should automatically trust you in real life." Palmer gestured wildly as he walked.

"You're right. You don't have to trust me, Palmer. At the moment, I don't plan on taking you to Coldston. There's more to this than his wanting one of his Thieves back. There are other Thieves on Beasor who don't have a problem with stealing souls, or other things." Chal soothed Palmer's worries.

As much as he wished he could trust Chal completely, Palmer couldn't bring himself to do that. Look what had happened the last time he'd trusted someone not to hurt him. He'd ended up trapped in a beautiful room and tormented until he either broke or managed to escape. At least his honour was still intact.

"Does it make me seriously confused or twisted that I can't trust you with all my secrets, yet I'm more than willing to share my body with you?" He ran his hands through his hair, tugging on the ends as he moved.

Chal snorted. "I don't think it makes you either of those things. It shows you have some sense. There are different levels of trust, and, to be honest, our minds are less likely to forget than our bodies."

Frowning, Palmer peered at Chal. "What the hell does that mean?"

"Our minds remember all the bad and good things done to us, but our bodies don't care about that shit. All they're interested in is the euphoria produced by good sex. By being ruled by our bodies, we're less like to make good judgement calls. Difficult to think straight when your cock's stiff and aching."

Palmer stood his ground when Chal climbed to his feet and walked up to him. Chal rested his hands on Palmer's shoulders and smiled.

"Having sex and making love are two different things. Making love requires a great deal of trust on all levels. Having sex is fun between two consenting adults, and there doesn't have to be a whole lot of trust between them." Chal leant forward and brushed their noses together. "I'll tell you a secret, Palmer. I kind of hope we get to the point where we're making love and not just having sex."

Palmer's mouth went dry, and he swayed closer to Chal. God, how could he stay strong when Chal seemed to be a silver-tongued deity sent to tempt him? The Tramp gave him a quick peck on the lips before backing up.

"I don't want to know where your files are. Keep those as a safety net, but I would like to know some of the other things you've seen Coldston do. While you're telling me all of this, I'm going to try to figure out exactly what Coldston wants. Maybe, between the two of us, we'll find a way to keep you safe from him without you having to hide here on Earth."

"Good," Palmer said. "I don't really like it here. Not that I know much about Beasor, but at least it's home and there are others like me there. I'd like to have a life with friends and a job I enjoy. Not being locked inside a room, and never being talked to by anyone because you didn't do what the boss wanted."

Chal muttered something under his breath, and Palmer couldn't make out what he said. He let the Tramp lead him back to the couch, where they sat, arms wrapped around each other. Palmer slowly told Chal everything he knew about Coldston and how the man operated.

He still didn't quite understand why he'd chosen to tell Chal everything instead of simply running the moment he'd first seen the Tramp. Aside from Coldston, Palmer had never trusted anyone. Being abandoned by his parents had formed doubt in his heart—he'd never believed anyone would stick around for long. Even though he'd gone with Coldston, and worked for him, Palmer had been anticipating the moment when Coldston would either throw him out or leave him.

Of course, Palmer had been the one to leave, not Coldston, but in a way the man had abandoned him by asking him to do something that would have broken his spirit. Any trust Palmer had had for Coldston was gone, and all he wanted was to be left alone.

His voice gave out after talking for two hours straight about all the evil things Coldston had done. After standing, Chal went to the kitchen and brought back a glass of water. He handed it to Palmer.

"Drink this," Chal ordered.

Palmer did, and his throat felt better. Yet his head pounded from all the stress and emotion of the day. He rubbed his forehead, wishing the pain would stop long enough for him to think clearly.

Chal held out his hand. "Why don't you go and try to sleep? It's been a long day, and a lot has happened. A good night's rest will help with your headache, and maybe things will be better in the morning."

"I don't know about that," Palmer muttered. "I think things might have gotten worse now that you're here. That means Coldston can find me at any moment."

"True, but I'll be here to help you if he does come."

Palmer put his hand in Chal's, letting the Tramp pull him to his feet. "Can I trust you to keep me safe? How do I know you won't leave me when Coldston shows up to take me? He did pay you to find and bring me home."

"True." Chal grinned and brought him closer. "But I get to keep my money regardless, whether I do the job or not."

Palmer huffed. "What about your reputation? Coldston could ruin you and you'd never get another job again."

Chal shrugged while leading Palmer over to the mattress resting on the floor. "I don't need to work anymore. I've made more than enough money to retire, if I wanted."

"Why haven't you, then?" Palmer climbed under the blankets and curled on his side, strangely happy when Chal sat next to him on the bed.

"I get bored, and working gives me stuff to do. I like travelling to new universes, and seeing new things." Chal trailed his fingers over Palmer's cheek. "Also, I guess, since I don't have anyone waiting for me at home, it's easy to go from job to job. Keeps me from getting lonely."

Palmer closed his eyes, letting Chal's touch soothe him. "Don't you have any friends? Or a boyfriend?"

"Do you really think I'd be kissing you if I had a boyfriend?"

Peering through his eyelashes, Palmer saw the scowl on Chal's face. He rested his hand on Chal's thigh.

"Not really, but I had to ask. What about friends? I'm sure you have some of those."

Chal snorted, then laughed. "Yes, I do actually have some friends. One of them owns the bar I hang out at, and his lover is a Gypsy. I'm also friends with a Thief who has to be one of the worst Thieves I've ever met."

"What do you mean by that?" Palmer frowned, trying to figure it out.

"Well, Steril should be related to you in some way, I swear. He doesn't believe in stealing anything. Doesn't matter whether it's a soul or just some object. I think his father is someone high up in the Thieves' Council."

"What are the Councils like?" Palmer vaguely remembered hearing about them when he was in school. After he stopped going, no one on the streets discussed the Councils except to warn against crossing them.

The Tramp slid back to rest against the pillows, and Palmer moved closer, placing his cheek on Chal's thigh. Chal stroked his hand over Palmer's face, and Palmer sighed, loving the tenderness of his touch.

"They're just a bunch of pretentious old men who believe they're more important than the rest of us peons." Chal curled his lip in disgust.

"They aren't? Even though they're the heads of their Councils and are members of the Supreme Council?" Palmer asked.

"No. Nothing makes them any better than the rest of us. Hell, I'm more powerful than the Head of the Tramps' Council, and Isaac knows it. It's the reason why I can get the contracts I want, and the percentages I want. He's afraid, if he doesn't give them to me, I'll lobby to take his place." Chal chuckled. "Little does he know, I want nothing to do with any of the Councils."

"Why not? It would give you something to do, since you don't need to work or anything," Palmer pointed out.

"Too much politics. I don't deal well with others on even the most impersonal level. I have very low tolerance for people kissing up to me, and that's what happens when you're a member of the Councils. People will tell you anything they think you want to hear as long as it gets them something in the end."

Palmer rolled over and sat up, the blankets pooling around his waist. He tugged off his shirt before turning back to Chal. The Tramp's interested gaze warmed Palmer, and he blushed.

"I'm hot," he explained.

"Yes, you are." Chal winked, but didn't continue teasing him.

"Shut up." Palmer smacked Chal in the chest.

Chal grabbed his hand and yanked him closer. Palmer gasped as their chests hit with a thud, and Chal encircled Palmer's waist with his arm. Their lips crashed together, causing Palmer to moan.

The sweep of Chal's tongue into Palmer's mouth drew a whimper from Palmer. Chal gripped the nape of Palmer's neck, tilting him in an angle to give them the deepest kiss possible. Palmer took his cues from Chal while their tongues duelled and Chal nibbled on Palmer's bottom lip.

God, he didn't care if the Tramp ended up handing him over to Coldston tomorrow, or whatever happened. Tomorrow would come whether Palmer wanted it to or not, but getting the chance to live one of his dreams might not happen again.

He fumbled with the buttons of Chal's shirt, trying to get it open so he'd be able to touch Chal's chest and play with his nipples. Eventually, the Tramp would end up naked, and Palmer would be able to wrap his lips around Chal's cock—if everything went according to the plan Palmer had in his head.

"Why did we dream about each other?" Chal whispered against Palmer's lips.

"Are you sure we did? Maybe we simply dreamt about a Tramp and a Thief." Palmer pushed the edges of Chal's shirt apart, and leant forward to lick a line from one hard nipple to the other.

Shifting slightly, Chal cradled Palmer's face in his hands and lifted his chin until their gazes met. "No, I'm sure it was you. Steril is the only other Thief I interact with regularly, and I wouldn't be dreaming about him."

Palmer's body wasn't really interested in the conversation, but his mind and heart were, so he had to ask, "Why not?"

Chal chuckled. "I'm not sure. He's cute as hell, and really nice, but I don't know. He just seems damaged in some way."

Palmer pulled away from Chal and stripped the Tramp's shirt off, leaving him a wide expanse of tanned skin to play with.

"Damaged in what way?" he asked, distracted by the sight of Chal sprawled under him, offered up like a sacrifice.

He leant forward, and took one of Chal's nipples between his teeth. Chal groaned as Palmer tugged on it gently.

"I'm not sure," Chal panted, seemingly determined to finish the conversation. "He doesn't seem happy with his life on Beasor. I wouldn't be surprised if he tries to run off."

Suddenly, Palmer rocked back on his heels and stared at Chal. "Why are we talking about some guy who isn't even here?"

Chapter Six

"You're right. Why are we talking about Steril?"

Chal reached out and grabbed Palmer's face, kissing him hard. He couldn't believe he'd got stuck talking about Steril when he was in bed with a more than willing man. Chal angled Palmer's face and took the kiss deeper. He sucked on Palmer's tongue, drawing moans from the young Thief.

He eased away a few inches and smiled at Palmer. "I think we need to lose some clothes."

"Okay."

Palmer nodded eagerly, tearing Chal's shirt off and diving for the button of Chal's pants. Chal let him go, happy to know Palmer was as into this as he was. Soon they were both naked, and Chal rolled them over so Palmer was under him.

He rocked their hips together, biting his lip at how amazing the touch of Palmer's skin on his felt. Chal wanted to bury himself deep inside Palmer, claiming the man as his. He paused, confused at where the possessive feelings came from.

Chal had never cared enough about any guy to want to claim him. Not even Weston, and hell, they'd even lived together for a while. There had also never been the overwhelming need to keep Weston safe from every bad thing life could throw at them. Yet here Chal was, wanting and needing to wrap Palmer in cotton wool and protect him from the world.

They rubbed their erections against each other and they both groaned. The room was warm, and soon their skin was coated by a fine sheen of sweat. Chal pinched one of Palmer's nipples between his finger and thumb, and Palmer gasped.

"Do you like that?" Chal murmured.

Palmer nodded, and Chal laughed.

"It feels a lot different in real life than it did in the dreams, doesn't it?"

"Yes," Palmer whispered, obviously caught up in the sensations of Chal's touch.

Chal didn't say anything else. He concentrated on stoking Palmer's lust—he wanted the Thief to completely forget everything except Chal and how he made him feel. He trailed his lips along the line of Palmer's neck, nibbling and sucking as he went.

Palmer squirmed and whimpered, and each sound encouraged Chal to continue. He replaced his fingers on Palmer's nipple with his lips, taking the hard nub of flesh between his teeth and tugging slightly.

"Oh!" Palmer buried his fingers in Chal's hair and held him close, not letting Chal move away.

Chal fought for enough freedom to move to his other nipple, so it wouldn't be neglected. While he teased Palmer with his mouth, Chal slid his hands down Palmer's sides to his hips. He urged the Thief to spread his legs even more, and, when he did, Chal settled between his thighs.

"Put your hands above your head," Chal ordered, breathing the words against Palmer's chest.

"Why?"

"Don't worry. I'm not going to do anything you don't like."

Palmer did as Chal told him, setting his hands above his head, fisting the sheets under him. Chal pushed up onto his knees and stared at the desire-inducing picture Palmer made, stretched out below him.

Palmer's cock wasn't as long or fat as Chal's, but it was a good length, and Chal couldn't wait to feel it in his mouth. He scooted down, wedging his shoulders between Palmer's thighs. He licked his lips when he got an up-close-and-personal view of Palmer's dick.

Chal blew out a puff of hot air, bathing Palmer in it. Palmer's penis twitched and another soft moan filled the room around them. Chal placed his hands on Palmer's hips, pinning him to the mattress before he licked a line from the base of Palmer's shaft to the spongy tip.

Palmer cried out, but Chal kept him from shooting off the bed. Chal swallowed Palmer down, relaxing his muscles to take him in as far as possible. He hummed when the head of Palmer's cock hit the back of his throat. Chal preferred to receive blow jobs, not give them, but something told him he'd probably end up enjoying pleasuring Palmer this way.

The sounds of joy coming from Palmer let Chal know he was doing it right. He applied more suction when he pulled off, and pressed the tip of his tongue into Palmer's slit. Chal slipped one of his hands down to cup Palmer's balls in a firm grip. He squeezed gently while sucking on Palmer's dick like a candy cane.

When Palmer was pretty much babbling incoherently, Chal moved his hand down to rub his finger over Palmer's opening. The Thief shuddered at the contact, but didn't pull away. In fact, he pressed against Chal, seeming to ask for more.

He let Palmer slide out of his mouth and looked up to meet Palmer's lust-dazed gaze.

"Do you have lube?"

Palmer blinked a few times, and Chal could tell he was trying to get his brain working through all the need and want.

"Yes. In the nightstand." Palmer waved in the general direction of the table next to the bed.

"Don't move." Chal patted Palmer's hip while crawling over to the edge and reaching for the drawer.

"I don't think I can, and you haven't even fucked me yet," Palmer admitted.

Chal chuckled. "Just wait. I'll blow your mind."

Palmer pinched Chal's ass. "I'm hoping you will. Maybe I'll be walking funny tomorrow."

"Got it." Chal held up the tube and rolled back to Palmer. "At least you'll know I fucked you in the morning. You'll be feeling it."

Palmer blushed, but didn't comment. He brought his knees up to his chest, exposing his hole to Chal's gaze. His mouth went dry at the implied trust Palmer showed him by doing that. Nothing made a man more vulnerable than offering up the most private part of his body for a lover.

He popped the top of the lube and squirted some on his fingers. He set it aside, knowing he would need it when Palmer was ready to take him. As he positioned his finger at Palmer's entrance, he glanced up at him.

"Have you done this before? I need to know because I don't want to hurt you or anything."

Palmer's face turned a darker red, but he answered, "Twice. I've done the other stuff more, but I've only had sex twice. The guys I was with didn't like kissing, though. It's hard to get away from Coldston's watch dogs long enough to find someone to fuck me."

Chal didn't want to talk about Coldston. Some part of his brain was telling him that having sex with Palmer wasn't very professional. Yet Chal didn't really care, because it wasn't like he was going to turn Palmer over to the bastard anyway. From the moment he'd met the Thief, he'd known Coldston had fed him a line of bull about Palmer stealing anything from him.

"Okay. Thanks for being honest."

He eased the tip of one finger in, pressing through the tight ring of muscles. Chal looked up to see Palmer bite his bottom lip.

"You're really tight. I'll try to take it as slowly as possible," Chal promised.

Palmer shook his head. "No. Don't treat me like I'm fragile. I can take whatever you give me."

Chal wasn't entirely sure about that, but he understood what Palmer was saying. Without rushing, he continued to push his finger in. When Palmer finally relaxed, Chal retreated and returned with a second finger. Palmer accepted them without too much resistance, and Chal began pumping them in and out. He wanted Palmer as stretched and relaxed as possible before he took him.

He twisted his fingers, and Palmer almost levitated. He laughed softly as Palmer begged him to do that again. It appeared that Palmer was a talker during sex. Chal didn't mind. He liked knowing his lover was enjoying himself.

"More. Please, Chal. I need more," Palmer pleaded.

Chal was more than happy to give the Thief whatever he wanted. He found the lube with his free hand while he continued to prepare Palmer. After managing to get the tube open one-handed, Chal got his cock coated with very little mess.

"Are you ready, Palmer?"

Palmer pushed up on his elbows and glared at Chal. "If I was any more ready, I'd have come by now."

Chal blinked at the attitude. Seemed Palmer got a little snippy during sex as well. He'd have to remember that.

"All right."

He removed his fingers and placed the head of his cock at Palmer's opening. Chal started pushing in, and Palmer gasped. Chal stroked his hands along his lover's chest and sides, working on easing him.

"Keep breathing, honey. This will go better if you can relax. It's been a long time, and I'm not a small guy."

Palmer met Chal's gaze, and the Tramp watched as he visibly took a deep breath and his inner channel suddenly seemed to suck Chal in.

"That's perfect."

Praising him, Chal slid all the way in and froze. He'd wait as long as it took for Palmer to get used to being so full. Palmer grimaced and shifted slightly, causing Chal to bite his lip. The brush of skin against skin made Chal want to start thrusting.

He wasn't prepared for Palmer reaching up and popping him in the shoulder.

"What the hell was that for?"

"Are you going to fuck me or did you fall asleep or something?"

"Geez, honey. You're pretty pushy for not having much experience." Chal winked while he slid all but the tip of his cock out. "Brace yourself. It's going to be hard and fast."

Palmer lifted his arms above his head and pressed them against the headboard. "Go ahead and take me as hard as you want. Like I said, I'm not fragile."

Chal took him at his word. He gripped Palmer's hips and hammered into him, driving cries of pleasure from Palmer with each thrust. Palmer wrapped his legs around Chal's waist, digging his heels into his ass. They moved together like they'd been making love for centuries instead of it being their first time.

After sliding his hands under Palmer to grip his ass, Chal lifted his hips to deepen the angle of his thrusts. He nailed Palmer's gland and the Thief shouted.

"Oh, my God." Palmer whimpered, tightening his thighs around Chal.

Chal grunted, but couldn't catch his breath enough to say anything. All he could think about was taking Palmer and spilling his seed in him, claiming him in the most primal way. He hadn't thought it possible, but he sped up, pumping in and out as fast as he possibly could.

He watched as Palmer wrapped his hand around his cock and started stroking in time with Chal. The feel of Palmer's tight ass surrounding his dick and the sight of Palmer jerking himself off combined to bring Chal's climax crashing over him.

Slamming deep into Palmer, he flooded his lover's passage with hot cum. Palmer shuddered and cum spilled from him to coat his stomach and hand. Their separate yells mingled, filling the room with the sounds of their release.

Chal rolled to the side when his arms threatened to collapse. Palmer groaned as Chal slid from him, and Chal laid his hand on Palmer's chest.

"Are you okay? I wasn't too rough, was I?"

Palmer laughed, sounding exhausted. "I'm fine, though I'm going to have to figure out how to get out of bed and into the bathroom. I have to clean up, or I'm going to be sticky."

It was then that Chal realised he hadn't used any protection. He winced, and braced his body on his elbow so he could look down at Palmer.

"I'm sorry, honey. I didn't even think about using a rubber. I was so eager to get inside you." He rubbed his hand over Palmer's stomach.

"Don't worry about it, Chal. For some reason Coldston had me vaccinated against all diseases. Not sure why. Maybe he thought he'd pimp me out or something." Palmer patted Chal's face. "I'm proud of the fact I made you forget about a condom."

"Thank God. I got the same vaccination, but I wasn't sure if you had or not, and I didn't want to make you think I was the kind of guy who didn't take care of his partner like that."

"Admittedly, I don't know much about you, considering we just met, but I'm trusting my gut here, and saying you're not that guy. You got carried away. That's all, and there's nothing to worry about." Palmer grimaced when he shifted on the mattress. "Well, aside from cleaning up before our cum dries."

Chuckling, Chal climbed off the bed, and offered his hand to help Palmer stand. They went to the bathroom where they washed off before going back and stripping the blankets from the mattress. Once it was remade, Palmer crawled under the covers and Chal joined him. They spooned, with Palmer's back against Chal's chest. Chal laid his hand over Palmer's heart, feeling it beat beneath his palm.

He drifted to sleep, listening to the sound of Palmer breathing.

* * * *

Palmer opened his eyes and stared at the wall across from him. He frowned, trying to figure out why he was on that side of the bed when he normally slept on the other side. The warm body behind him gave him a clue, along with the ache in his ass and muscles.

He wiggled, wanting to roll over and look at Chal. He'd never slept with anyone before. Slept as in sharing a bed while they were both asleep, and not having sex. It was strange, but he found he didn't mind it. Chal tightened his embrace, pulling Palmer even closer to him.

Palmer settled back down, absorbing the odd way being held by Chal made him feel. For some reason, the Tramp created a haven of safety for Palmer, and he hadn't felt like that since the day his parents had abandoned him. It was the thing he'd been searching for when Coldston had found him.

The bastard had promised he'd keep Palmer safe and that he'd have a home where he'd be loved for who he was, but, of course, Coldston had lied. Palmer had discovered the perfidy within days of moving to Coldston's compound.

Coldston had preyed on Palmer's weaknesses and needs, using them to get the Thief to do what he wanted. To Palmer's shame, it wasn't until Coldston had asked him to steal a man's soul that Palmer drew the line and said no more. He wasn't going to kill a man just so Coldston could make more money.

"You're thinking too hard for so early in the morning," Chal murmured in his ear.

"Sorry. I didn't mean to wake you." Palmer tried to relax, but, now that he'd thought about Coldston, he couldn't get him out of his head.

"It's all right." Chal smoothed circles over Palmer's chest and stomach. "What's got you so tense?"

"Coldston and why he keeps chasing me," he admitted.

"So you're having a nightmare, huh?" Chal nuzzled Palmer's ear. "I could take your mind off your problems."

Palmer wormed his way around, so they were facing each other. "But it wouldn't stop them from being there when we were done."

Chal nodded. "True, but do we have to come up with a solution right this moment? Coldston will still be there when we get up in the morning."

"I can't help it. I've spent most of my life worried about what he was going to do. It's even worse since I've run away from him."

He dropped his gaze to Chal's chest, intrigued by the darker nipples on the Tramp's pectoral muscles. Palmer scraped a thumbnail over one of them, causing it to harden. Chal rumbled low in his throat, and suddenly Palmer didn't want to talk about Coldston. He wanted to find out how Chal tasted.

Leaning forward, he placed his lips over Chal's nipple and flicked it with his tongue. Chal jolted like he'd been shocked, and Palmer smiled, happy he could get a reaction from the man. With a gentle push, he got Chal to roll over onto his back, and he followed him, not letting up on tormenting Chal's nipples. Chal entwined his fingers in Palmer's hair, appearing unwilling to let him go. Not that he was interested in leaving anytime soon, or quitting for that matter.

He switched from one to the other, nibbling and sucking until each nub was red and wet. Whimpering, Chal exerted a little pressure, encouraging Palmer to slide lower. This time, Palmer was ready to do that. He trailed kisses and gentle love bites down the centre of Chal's chest and stomach, taking a moment to tease his lover's belly button.

"Palmer, quit messing around," Chal complained. The Tramp lifted his hips, brushing Palmer's chest with his erection.

Palmer shivered at the pre-cum painting a line over his skin. Would Chal let Palmer fuck him, or was the man strictly a top? Palmer had never fucked anyone. He'd always been the one to offer up his ass, and it had never occurred to him before this to want to do it. Yet there was something about Chal that made Palmer want to fill him with his own cum, to claim Chal the same way that Chal had claimed him.

He reached down between Chal's legs and ran his fingers along Chal's crease, stopping to rub his thumb over his hole. Moaning, Chal spread his thighs, silently offering Palmer whatever he wanted.

"Will you let me fuck you?" He had to ask, even as he pressed against Chal's opening.

"Oh, God yes." Chal's dark brown eyes met Palmer's and he saw the sincerity in the Tramp's gaze. "I love getting fucked as much as I like doing the fucking."

He couldn't control the smile bursting across his face. Palmer shot up to crush his lips into Chal's, demanding the man open to him. Chal didn't protest, doing exactly what Palmer wanted. Palmer slid his tongue in and duelled with Chal's for a minute before he pulled away.

"Where did we put the lube?" He glanced around.

Chal gestured towards the nightstand. "It's over there. I didn't put it away because I was hoping we'd have another go before morning."

Palmer shot across the bed and snatched up the slick. While he was busy, Chal flipped over onto his hands and knees. Palmer almost swallowed his tongue when he turned to see that firm ass presented so perfectly for him. He smoothed his hand over one tight globe and squeezed.

Grunting, Chal pushed back into his hand and Palmer grinned. He drew his hand back and slapped Chal hard. The Tramp jumped, but didn't say a word. As much as Palmer liked the look of his handprint marking Chal's ass, he had other things to think about.

He spread Chal's cheeks apart and leant forward to blow a soft puff of air over Chal's hole. A shiver worked its way over Chal's body, and Palmer knew he'd enjoyed that. Without saying anything, he licked a line from the top of Chal's crease to right behind the man's balls.

"Holy shit," Chal shouted.

Palmer didn't talk. He'd had one lover who'd played with him like that, and he remembered how crazy it had driven him. He wanted to do that to Chal before he fucked him. He settled down to stretch Chal with his tongue and fingers, doing everything in his power to drive Chal out of his mind.

It wasn't long before Chal was reduced to incoherent noises, with no words distinguishable. He simply grunted and moaned, undulating under Palmer's touch. Palmer speared him with his tongue, loosening the ring of muscle guarding Chal's most private place. He pushed three fingers inside, twisting and pumping until he hit Chal's gland.

"Fuck!" Chal arched, shoving back and begging for more. "Please, Palmer. I need you to fuck me right now. I can't take much more of this and I want to come with you inside me."

Palmer rocked back on his heels. "All right."

He popped open the lube, coated his own cock before squirting some over Chal's opening. Rising up on his knees, he placed the head of his dick at Chal's hole. He slowly started pushing in, taking his time, even though Chal kept trying to take him in faster than he wanted.

"Take it easy, Chal. I don't want to hurt you," he informed the Tramp.

"I don't care. I don't mind a little pain with my pleasure. You're taking too damn long to fuck me, honey." Chal glanced over his shoulder, his eyes glazed with passion and need. "I want you buried so deep inside me I can feel you in my throat."

Palmer didn't really think that was possible, but it wasn't the time for discussing that. He took the Tramp at his word, gripped Chal's hips and slammed into him. Palmer let his head drop back as he absorbed how tight and hot Chal was. Holy shit, it was like his dick was in a vice — but in the best way possible.

Chal shoved back, getting his attention. "Move, damn it. Fuck me as hard as you can."

"All right."

Palmer began to hammer in and out of Chal, revelling in the way the sounds of their bodies slapping together filled the room, along with the scent of sex and sweat. His climax built at the base of his spine, but exploded through the rest of his body.

"Chal," he shouted as he came, flooding the Tramp with his cum.

Chal grunted, obviously not able to say anything as he spilled his own cum on the sheets beneath him. Palmer's strength gave out on him and he folded over, covering Chal's back. Chal managed to brace himself enough to get both of them on their sides while they tried to catch their breath.

When he could finally form words again, Palmer stroked Chal's side and murmured, "Are you okay?"

"I think my brain exploded or something," Chal muttered and laughed.

"That's a good thing, right?"

Chal wiggled around until he looked directly at Palmer. He studied him for a moment. "You've never topped before, have you?"

Palmer shrugged, dropping his gaze to Chal's chest. "No. Admittedly, I don't have a lot of experience, but both times I bottomed. I hope I did okay."

Chal grinned, and embraced Palmer. "Honey, you did more than okay. You can fuck me any time you want."

Pride surged through Palmer, and he kissed Chal, putting all his happiness into it. Chal kissed him back, pulling Palmer closer to him. Time was lost as they kissed and touched, not trying to build desire again, just simply learning how each other felt.

After a while, Palmer pulled away and smiled. "We should clean up again before we fall asleep."

They repeated their earlier washing before they cuddled under the blankets. This time it was Palmer who fell asleep to the sound of Chal breathing.

* * * *

Palmer's front door slamming open woke them up and they sat, staring at the man standing in the middle of the room. Palmer cringed when he recognised the Tramp. It was one of Coldston's enforcers. Chal swore and climbed out of bed, scrambling to tug on his pants. Palmer did the same thing, all the while not taking his eyes off the Tramp who'd busted in on them.

"Time to head back to the boss, Palmer. All this little bid for freedom got you was a pissed-off boss."

"Who the fuck are you?" Chal challenged the other man.

"Since you weren't doing your job, Coldston sent me after Palmer. I'm dragging his ass back to Beasor where the boss will take care of him."

Chapter Seven

Chal glared at the man standing in front of them. How dare Coldston send someone to follow him? Yet he wasn't surprised the bastard didn't trust him to do his job.

The stranger grinned at Palmer, but there wasn't any sign of friendliness — or even emotion — in his smile.

Shivering, Palmer edged closer to Chal and took his hand. Good, because Chal didn't plan on sticking around any longer. He should've taken Palmer back to Beasor the moment he found him. Not to give to Coldston, but to be on his own turf with friends he could go to for help. Well, he'd just do that now.

Without giving any sign or saying anything, Chal whirled and embraced Palmer. He closed his eyes, thinking of Alden and Percy's apartment. He just hoped he didn't pop in on them at an inappropriate moment. The thug shouted, but it was too late. Chal was a Tramp, and he didn't need any preparation time to be able to flash between the universes. Even though the other Beasor was a Tramp as well, Chal had discovered he could flash faster than most other Tramps, and the Beasor had no idea where Chal was taking Palmer.

It was the only thing that made Tramps special. It certainly wasn't their looks or intelligence.

"What the fuck?"

Chal opened his eyes to find Alden staring at him, mouth open in shock. His friend stood in the middle of the living room, wearing a towel and nothing else. Chal winked.

"Just thought I'd drop in to see how you're doing. Looking real good there, Alden."

"Chal, what the hell are you doing? You can't just pop in like that. And who do you have with you?" Alden glared at him, arms crossed over his chest.

"Palmer," Chal exclaimed. "Are you all right?"

He eased his hold on the Thief, and looked down at him. Palmer's eyes were squeezed shut like he was afraid to open them. His skin was pale and he trembled. Chal led him over to the couch, getting him to sit.

"It's all right, Palmer. You can open your eyes. I brought you to a friend's place. I wouldn't have turned you over to Coldston, not after sleeping with you. What kind of asshole do you take me for?"

Palmer peeked through his eyelashes at Chal, obviously trying to reassure himself that Chal was telling the truth. He grinned at the Thief, hoping they'd established some trust. When Palmer opened both eyes, and glanced around, Chal laughed as Palmer's gaze landed on Alden and widened.

"He is rather good-looking for an ordinary Beasor, isn't he?" Chal mock-whispered. "But, unfortunately, he's taken by a rather possessive Gypsy, and has been for several years now. No hope for either of us, I'm afraid."

"Shut up, Chal. I'm going to get dressed, then you can tell me why you're sitting in my living room with a Thief."

They watched Alden disappear down the hallway. After his friend disappeared, Chal turned to find Palmer looking at him.

"How did we get here?"

Chal laughed. "I flashed us here. You're probably going to feel a little tired and weak. Even flashing with a Tramp can sap you."

Blinking, Palmer slumped against Chal and yawned. "I am tired. Why did you bring us here?"

"I wasn't going to let him lay a hand on you, and this was the first place I thought to take you. I doubt Coldston will think of looking here for you. You should be safe until I can contact someone about your case."

He jerked when Palmer clung to him.

"You're leaving me here with people I don't know?"

The panic in Palmer's voice drew a grunt from Chal. He hadn't expected him to react like that. He cradled Palmer's face in his hands, and studied the Thief's face.

"Honey, I'll be around all the time, but Coldston will be able to find out where I live, and you'll be vulnerable there. Staying here is better. The apartment is over Alden's pub. There are people in and out all the time." Chal rubbed his thumbs over Palmer's cheekbones. "Trust me. It'll be far safer for you here than at my place."

"All right, Chal. Tell me what you're doing here at ten in the morning without letting us know you were coming." Alden returned to the room.

Chal wrapped his arm around Palmer's shoulder, bringing the Thief closer to him. "I had to get Palmer away from the Tramp who'd come to take him back to Coldston."

"First things first." Alden held out his hand to Palmer. "I'm Alden Sparks. It's nice to meet you."

"I'm Palmer Holmes."

They shook hands, but Chal could see Palmer was still nervous. He grunted softly. He couldn't really blame Palmer for being slightly freaked out. One moment they were lying in bed, enjoying the blissful aftermath of their climaxes. Next, they were half naked, sitting in a stranger's living room.

When that thought hit him, Chal glanced over at Alden. "Can Palmer and I borrow some shirts? We had to leave in a hurry."

"Sure. Palmer, would you like to wash up while I get Chal those shirts?"

Palmer nodded. "Yes, please."

"Come with me." Alden gestured for the Thief to follow him.

Chal stayed seated. He couldn't hover protectively over Palmer. He might have promised to keep him safe, but Palmer didn't really need him to be with him twenty-four-seven. It just wouldn't work.

Alden returned to the living room, and tossed a shirt at Chal. "Here's one of mine. I left one of Percy's in the bathroom for Palmer."

"Thanks. We barely had time to get our pants on." Chal slid the T-shirt on. When he lifted his head, he found Alden glaring at him.

"Did you fuck him?"

Chal tensed, not liking Alden's tone. "What if I did?"

"Jesus, Chal, he's just a kid. Probably doesn't know anything about the world. Where the hell did you find him?" Alden shoved his hand through his hair and paced.

"Well, first of all, Palmer's older than he looks, and trust me, he knows about the world. I found him on Earth. He's my job."

"Is fucking him part of the job?"

"What? Hell no." Chal shook his head. "I don't mess around with my clients, or innocents."

Alden stopped in front of him, and propped his fists on his hips. "Then what the hell happened? Why this one?"

It was his turn to jump to his feet and pace from one end of the room to the other. He discovered he didn't have a good answer for Alden. It was true that he'd broken one of his most important rules about business and pleasure. Yet he wasn't upset or disappointed by his actions.

"I've been dreaming about him for the past couple of months," he admitted.

Alden frowned. "Dreaming of him? What do you mean? Are you sure it's Palmer you were dreaming of, and not some random Thief? They do look a lot alike."

Chal met Alden's gaze. "Does Percy look like every other Gypsy?"

"What? No, he doesn't."

"To you, Percy doesn't look like every other Gypsy, but to most other people he does. It's the same with Palmer and me. I could tell which one he was in a crowd of Thieves."

"Why have you been dreaming about him?" Alden shook his head.

Shrugging, Chal said, "I don't know. Like I said, I started dreaming about him a couple of months ago.

Before I even took this job. The moment I saw him in the diner, I knew he was the one I'd been kissing in my dreams."

Alden was quiet, and Chal didn't break the silence while he listened to the sound of the shower from Alden's bathroom.

"Where's Percy?" He'd just realised the Gypsy hadn't made an appearance yet, and that wasn't like Percy, not with all the excitement going on.

Alden grinned. "He and his sister had a shopping date."

Chal rolled his eyes, but he laughed. "I'm not surprised. I'm also not shocked you chose to stay home."

"I'm not dumb. I'd end up carrying all their bags, and those two can shop for hours. I don't have the endurance for that." Alden grimaced. "But don't try to change the subject. What the hell does your client want with Palmer?"

"I haven't figured it out yet."

Normally Chal wouldn't discuss his work with anyone, but he needed help, and he trusted Alden not to blab about it.

"It's not like Coldston couldn't find another Thief to work for him. They're all over the place, and most don't really care what they do or what harm they cause. There's more to this job than meets the eye." Chal scrubbed his hand over his chin.

The water shut off, and Alden studied Chal while they waited for Palmer to come and join them.

"I've never seen you like this. Are you seriously considering not returning Palmer to Coldston like you were hired to do?"

Chal looked at Alden and nodded. "Yes. I told Palmer I wouldn't give him to Coldston. Not now.

There's too much going on. Coldston has had Thieves steal people's souls and the law says it's murder. Palmer has evidence against Coldston, and the crimes he's committed. That's why I think the bastard wants him, though I do believe there's another reason that we don't know about."

The door opened and Palmer walked down the hallway to join them. Pride surged in Chal when Palmer went right to him, pressing as close as he could get. Chal slid his arm around Palmer's waist, bringing the Thief still closer to him.

Palmer rested his head on Chal's shoulder, and Alden watched them with a puzzled expression. Chal understood the confusion his friend was feeling, since it was the same kind he felt himself.

As much as Chal had wanted to find someone he could care for and have a relationship with, he'd never got so attached to a man as quickly as he'd become attached to Palmer. It usually took him far longer to trust someone. Maybe having dreamt of Palmer had helped him accept the Thief as a friend.

"Don't you think whoever Coldston sent has reported back to him?" Alden dropped into one of the chairs across from the couch. He motioned to the other furniture. "Why not take a seat?"

Chal escorted Palmer to the couch, and they sat together. Palmer practically entangled their legs and arms, trying to sit on Chal's lap.

"Won't Coldston come looking for you when he gets the news that you took Palmer away?"

Palmer shuddered, and Chal smoothed his hand down Palmer's back. He didn't really want to discuss it with Palmer around, but he also didn't want to exclude him when it came to his safety.

"He will, but I'm not worried about him. I'm more worried about what he wants with Palmer."

His phone vibrated in his pocket, and he managed to get it without letting go of Palmer. Scowling, he glanced at the screen to check the caller ID.

"Speak of the devil." He held up his phone. "I think I'll let it go to voicemail."

There was a soft beep when Coldston finished recording his message. Within seconds, the phone rang again. This time it was Isaac, and Chal sighed.

"I'm going to have to answer this at some point, but I don't want to be here when I do." Chal untangled himself from Palmer before turning to look at the Thief. "I have to get out of here before anyone figures out this is where I took you. I don't want to take a chance that Coldston will grab you while I'm out."

"I understand. I don't have to like it, but I get that you're doing this to keep me safe." Palmer brushed a kiss over Chal's cheek.

Chal kissed him back before turning to look at Alden. "I hate doing this to you, Alden, but can you look out for Palmer for a while, or just until I figure this out?"

Nodding, Alden stood. "Of course, we'll help you out. You went to a lot of trouble to help me find and rescue Percy. We owe you."

"You don't owe me anything. I was more than happy to help. Percy's my friend as well." Chal stood and went to hug Alden. "I'll try not to take too long, and hopefully, when I get back, Palmer won't have to worry about his life anymore."

"Percy and I will do our best to keep him safe while you're gone," Alden promised.

Chal gave Palmer one last kiss before he left, heading downstairs to the street. He'd go to one of his other apartments in the city. He'd set up several safe houses throughout Catalai, in case he ever needed to hide from anyone. Maybe it would have been smarter to take Palmer to one of those, but he didn't want to leave the Thief on his own.

It wasn't that he didn't believe Palmer wouldn't be able to take care of himself. Chal just preferred to have someone around in case Palmer needed help. He summoned a sled, and tried to ignore the vibrating phone in his pocket. He knew it was more than likely Coldston or Isaac, and he wasn't prepared to talk to either of them.

* * * *

Palmer sat on the couch, hands in his lap, and stared at Alden. The man was an ordinary Beasor by his looks, but he was still quite handsome. His nerves shot through him, and he wished he'd gone with Chal. Oh, he understood why Chal had left him here instead of taking him wherever he was going, yet he didn't know this man. It didn't matter if Chal trusted Alden or not.

"Umm...I'm not sure what we're supposed to be doing here." Palmer shrugged. "I don't have a lot of friends, or spend a lot of time with other people."

Alden chuckled. "I have to eat and head down to the pub. I have orders to place for the next month or so. You're welcome to come with me. It's not that exciting, but I think, until Percy comes home, you should be with someone at all times."

"Do you really think Coldston is going to come in and take me from here? Chal said he probably doesn't know where I am." Palmer rubbed his hands on his thighs.

"He doesn't know it at the moment, but, at some point, he'll figure it out. There are only a few places Chal goes when he's in Catalai." Alden stood and gestured to Palmer. "Let's have some breakfast, and you can see if you'd like to run a pub."

Palmer laughed. "To be honest, I don't think I've got the right temperament to run anything. I don't have a great track record on running my own life, that's for sure."

"Everyone screws up. It's a matter of learning from your mistakes, moving on from there, and trying not to repeat them. That's all anyone can do."

Palmer nodded, but he wasn't entirely convinced.

"Here, these are a pair of Percy's. They should fit you all right. We'll worry about getting you some of your own clothes when Percy comes back." Alden handed him a pair of shoes.

He slid them on, and they were a little big. He could deal with it for a while anyway. Alden went into the kitchen and started pulling food out of the refrigerator. Palmer joined him, and sat at the island counter out of Alden's way.

"Is there anything I can help you with?"

Alden shook his head. "No. I've got it covered. Just sit there and breathe. I bet it was pretty frightening when that guy showed up at your place."

Palmer nodded before he propped his chin on his hand. "Yes. Ruined the post-sex snuggle too."

Alden's snort caused Palmer to blush. He hadn't meant to say that. He understood how strange it must seem to Alden that Palmer would be willing to jump into bed with Chal, especially since Chal had been sent to take him back to Coldston. Palmer wished he could explain well enough to clear it up for Alden, but he couldn't. Mostly because he didn't have a good explanation.

"It does suck when snuggling gets interrupted," Alden commented.

"You must be wondering why Chal didn't take me back to Coldston the moment he found me," Palmer murmured.

Alden glanced at him over his shoulder where he stood by the stove. "I'm curious, but I figured Chal had his reasons for doing it. Might not have been the smartest move the Tramp ever made, but I think he can handle Coldston."

Thinking about Coldston caused Palmer to shudder. As much as he trusted Chal, and, to be honest, he trusted the Tramp far more than was intelligent, Palmer found he believed in Coldston's abilities to continue to ruin his life.

"Not that I want to disparage Chal, but I've seen what Coldston can do, and he's very vicious." Palmer swallowed, remembering a particularly disturbing beating he'd witnessed.

"I'm sure he is a bastard, but I think Chal will turn out to be smarter than he is." Alden dished up their breakfast and set the plate in front of Palmer. Alden poured two cups of coffee before joining him at the counter. "Admittedly, most Tramps aren't known for their brains, but Chal has surprised me several times with his ideas and plots."

Palmer shrugged. "I haven't known Chal as long as you have, so I guess I'll have to take your word for it. As much as I don't want to go back to Coldston, I don't want Chal hurt because of me."

Alden took a bite of his eggs and chewed. After he swallowed, he asked, "Did you dream about Chal?"

Palmer stared at the Beasor. "How did you know about that?"

"Chal told me he dreamt about you, which was why you ended up in bed together. Now, Chal can be a fast worker if he wants to, but lately he hasn't been interested in one-night stands or anything like that. Sort of surprised me when he said you were in bed together when Coldston's man arrived." Alden grinned at him.

His cheeks warmed and Palmer dropped his gaze to his plate. He wasn't sure what to say about that. It wasn't like he'd planned on seducing Chal to convince the Tramp to let him go. It had just sort of happened, and Palmer wasn't entirely sure there'd be a next time.

Not because he didn't want to do it again with Chal. Heck, if the Tramp showed up in the next minute and told him to strip, Palmer would do it without hesitation. He might have technically only met Chal a few days ago, but, in his soul, it felt like he'd known him forever.

He tensed when Alden reached across the table and patted his hand.

"I was teasing, though I do want to know if you did dream about Chal. I find it very interesting. Were they the same dreams or different?"

Palmer shrugged. "I'm not sure how alike they were. We didn't really talk about them. Just acknowledged them and jumped into bed."

"Sometimes when it's right, it's right."

Alden chuckled and Palmer glanced at him, noticing Alden wasn't really looking at him, but seemed to be remembering something. The other man met his gaze, and smiled.

"And sometimes, even though it's right, you take forever to tell the person you love them, because you don't want to screw up your friendship."

Palmer had the feeling Alden was talking about a situation he'd experienced personally.

"Hell, it only took me running away and getting kidnapped for both of us to come to our senses, but now I come home to find you entertaining a handsome man at our table."

The unexpected voice caused Palmer to shoot to his feet and whirl around. A Gypsy stood in the doorway, his shoulder braced against the frame and his arms crossed. If it wasn't for the twinkle in the man's lavender eyes, Palmer would have believed he really was angry.

He watched Alden walk around the table and stroll right into the Gypsy's personal space. They shared a heated kiss, and Palmer turned away, not wanting to watch the intimate embrace. He might not know Alden and Percy very well, but he could see how much they really loved each other. At least, he assumed the Gypsy was Percy. Alden didn't strike Palmer as the kind of man who would be kissing anyone except the man he loved.

"While Palmer is very cute, he can't hold a candle to you in my eyes," Alden said. "You can turn around now, Palmer."

He turned to face the couple, and both men looked well kissed. He smiled, wishing he shared such a connection to someone that all the love he felt for the man would spill out, no matter who might be in the room. Maybe Chal would be that guy, or, if not, once this whole problem with Coldston was taken care of, Palmer could find the right man for him.

"Palmer Holmes, this is my lover, Percy Harlow." Alden introduced them.

"Hello, Palmer. Where'd my boyfriend find you?" Percy winked as they shook hands.

"I'm not sure he really found me. I sort of appeared in your living room," he informed the Gypsy.

"Appeared? Like magic?" Percy glanced at Alden with a questioning lift of his eyebrows.

"Actually, Chal brought him here. They did show up while I was getting ready to head downstairs."

Percy dragged Palmer back to the table while Alden cleared the plates. The Gypsy sat down next to him and smiled.

"Where did Chal find you? I'm terribly intrigued by this whole thing."

Having those bright, lavender eyes stare at him made Palmer uncomfortable and he dropped his gaze to his hands, lying in his lap.

"Percy, love, tone it down a little bit. I don't think he's used to talking with anyone like you," Alden suggested from where he stood at the sink.

Percy reached over and patted Palmer's hand. "I'm sorry. It's just this is the first time Chal's ever really brought a guy to meet us. He usually picks them up in the bar downstairs and takes them home for the night."

"Percy." There was a warning tone in Alden's voice.

The Gypsy's eyes widened as he seemed to realise what he was saying. "Well, hell, that didn't come out right. Now I've just made Chal sound like a slut. He didn't pick up guys every night, and certainly none at all lately."

Palmer covered his mouth with his hand, hiding his smirk as Percy started to backpedal. He thought about putting the Gypsy out of his misery, but he wanted to see what else Percy was going to say.

"Maybe you should stop while you're ahead, Percy. Chal doesn't need help screwing things up. I'm sure, as they spend more time together, Palmer will figure out all of Chal's faults." Alden dried his hands and joined them at the table.

"How did you end up here? I didn't know he was dating anyone." Percy leaned into Alden's side, their connection very obvious.

"We aren't. Chal was hired by someone to find me." Palmer didn't go into any more detail. He was pretty sure Alden would fill Percy in on what was going on.

"Really? Why?" Percy fluttered his eyelashes. "Do you have another suitor that Chal will have to compete with for your attention?"

Palmer shuddered when he thought of Coldston as a potential boyfriend. "God, no. It's a business issue."

Before Percy could ask any more questions, Alden bumped the Gypsy's shoulder with his own.

"Did you find any deals?"

"I didn't, but Kiki got a crazy amount of bags. We almost had to get a separate sled just for her stuff." Percy wrinkled his nose in disgust.

"Why are you acting all put out? You've made me cart tons of bags up the stairs after one of your shopping excursions," Alden pointed out.

"True, but I didn't drag you all over town, and force you to watch me try on lingerie."

Alden snorted and Palmer chuckled while Percy glared at them.

"It's not funny. I think I'm scarred for life." Percy rubbed his eyes. "I might need to bleach my eyes."

"Why did she want your opinion? It's not like you know anything about women's lingerie." Alden eyed

Percy. "Unless there's something you haven't told me."

Percy stared at Alden for a moment, and Palmer could tell the Gypsy was trying to process what Alden had said. When the light bulb went on in Percy's head, he jumped to his feet and smacked Alden on the back of the head.

"I don't wear women's clothes, Alden Sparks." Percy stalked out of the kitchen.

"Shouldn't you go after him?" Palmer glanced at Alden before looking back towards the hallway where Percy had disappeared.

"No. Percy's just being dramatic. He's not really upset or anything." Alden gestured for Palmer to stand. "Let's go downstairs. Percy'll be down when he's done meditating."

"All right."

Palmer still wasn't convinced he needed to stay with Alden and Percy. They seemed like nice people, but he didn't want to intrude on their lives. Yet he had no idea how to leave at the moment. With no money, he couldn't even find another Tramp to take him back to Earth, though maybe returning there wouldn't be a good idea. Coldston would send someone else.

He went with Alden down to the pub. The Beasor nodded towards the office door.

"You should probably stay out of sight for a day or two. If Coldston figures out Chal hangs out here, he might have someone looking for you. While I don't mind having Thieves around, most tend to hang out at a club closer to the Training Facility. There are a few who come here, but not many, so you'll stand out."

Palmer entered the office while Alden continued towards the front of the pub. Sitting on the leather couch, he rested his elbows on his knees and scrubbed his face with his hands. How had all of this happened? He'd never understood why Coldston hadn't just dumped him or let him go. Why was he so important that Coldston was hunting him down after he'd run away?

Like Chal had said, there were hundreds of other Thieves out there, so, even though Palmer wasn't willing to do what Coldston wanted anymore, Coldston could have found someone else to take Palmer's place. Yet he never had and he wouldn't let Palmer go.

Maybe Chal could figure out how to free Palmer from Coldston's clutches. He'd let the Tramp have some time to do it, but he'd also work on his back-up plan, just in case Chal's idea didn't pan out.

Chapter Eight

Chal growled in frustration. He hadn't been able to go and see Palmer for that last couple of days because Coldston's men had been following him around Catalai non-stop, and it was starting to get on his nerves. Oh, he understood why Coldston was keeping tabs on him, but it was still annoying.

"Mr Farnsmith."

He glanced up from the table where he sat in a small coffee house. A very tall, muscle-bound man stood next to him, glowering.

"Yes?"

"You need to come with me."

"Really? Who said?" Chal was pretty sure Coldston had got tired of waiting, and had sent the brawn to bring him in.

"Mr Coldston would like to talk to you."

The man reached out to grab Chal's arm, but Chal shoved his chair back and stood. While he still had to look up several more inches to meet the man's gaze, he didn't yield.

"I'm not going anywhere with you. If Coldston wants to talk to me, I'll be at the restaurant where our first meeting took place. I'll be there around eleven tomorrow morning." Chal shook his head. "I might be many things, but I'm not stupid. I go with you now, and no one ever hears from me again. I know the kind of man your employer is."

"That might be true, but I don't have time to argue with you. You didn't do the job he hired you for, so he wants to talk to you." The man reached for Chal's arm again, and Chal stepped away.

He laughed. "You really believe I'll just calmly go with you?"

"I don't care whether it's calmly or not. You are coming with me."

"What's going on here?"

Chal turned to see Steril walking towards them. There was something different about the Thief, and Chal straightened up. Steril didn't even look at him, just kept those golden eyes on Chal's possible captor.

"I don't see where it's any of your business, Thief." The enforcer started to move in front of Chal, his hands already out to grab Steril. "You should know better than to interfere with something that has nothing to do with you."

Before the enforcer could touch Steril, two other men pushed by and surrounded him. The Beasor didn't get a chance to say anything as they dragged him out of the coffee house. Chal stood in shock for a moment, trying to figure out what had happened. He turned to glance at Steril.

"Who were they? Why are you here?"

Smiling, Steril gestured towards Chal's table. "Sit. You're lucky I happened to be thirsty, or else he probably would've kidnapped you. We'd never have heard from you again."

Chal frowned and sat. "I could've gotten away from him. All I would have had to do was flash to a different universe. He's just a regular Beasor, and wouldn't have been able to follow me."

"I'm pretty sure he had silk ropes, and was going to bind you with them before you could have flashed."

One of the waitresses dropped off Steril's coffee and he thanked her. He sipped it while Chal still stared at him.

"Who were those men with you?"

"My bodyguards-slash-escorts, I guess. My father got tired of me running away from the Facility, so he gave me an ultimatum. The only way I'm able to come and go as I please is if I take those guys with me. If I don't, or if I slip away from them, all privileges will be revoked, and I'll be held captive in the Facility's grounds." Steril grimaced.

Chal shook his head. "That's terrible. Who is your father and why can he do that?"

"If I was still underage, he'd have every right to confine me to the compound."

"But you're over eighteen. You're an adult and have the right to do whatever you want."

Steril snorted. "Maybe if I was a normal Beasor and didn't have the family I have, I could do that, but it's not my luck. My dad is very powerful, and he has a definite idea of what his only son should do."

The tone colouring Steril's voice made Chal want to pursue that topic, but the expression on his friend's face told him it wouldn't be welcomed. Chal turned back to Coldston.

"He's going to figure out where I stashed Palmer. I'm an idiot, and Alden and Percy might get in trouble because of me." Chal scrubbed his hands over his face. "What the hell do I do?"

"First, you and I will go to Alden's, and, while we're on our way, you can tell me what's going on."

Steril's bodyguards returned, and the four of them grabbed a sled to take them to Alden's pub. Along the way, Chal explained what had happened, and how he wasn't sure what to do about it. All he did know was he wasn't turning Palmer over to Coldston.

"Of course you aren't. I'd like to meet Palmer, and, once that's taken care of, we'll contact the Head Council. They need to know what Coldston has been doing, and, while there will always be people who take advantage of us magical Beasors, there are rules and laws to keep it in check."

Steril patted Chal's hand after his pronouncement. The Thief seemed quite sure they'd be able to keep Palmer safe. As much as Chal wanted to believe, he had a nagging feeling they hadn't heard the last of Coldston.

When they pulled up in front of Alden's pub, they climbed out to see a crowd of people standing on the sidewalk. Fear crept along Chal's spine, chilling him. Steril's bodyguards made a path through the people into the pub. What they saw there drew curses from Chal, and a gasp from Steril.

Most of the tables and chairs were broken, along with a majority of the bottles and glasses from behind the bar. Alden stood in the middle of the chaos talking to a security officer, while Percy leaned against the counter, sobbing into a handkerchief.

Steril headed straight to Alden while Chal made his way to Percy. He stopped in front of the Gypsy, who threw himself in Chal's arms when he noticed him.

Chal stroked Percy's blond hair, and murmured softly until Percy got his crying under control.

"Where's Palmer? Is he okay? Are you and Alden okay? I'm so sorry, Percy. I really didn't think this whole thing through."

Percy pressed his finger against Chal's lips. "We're fine, but I'm afraid they took Palmer. We tried to stop them, Chal. Really we did, but there were too many of them."

"And Alden needed to keep you safe. You're his first priority, Percy, and I don't blame him at all. I'll see what I can find out."

He walked over to Alden, keeping Percy with him. The police officer wandered off with Steril, seeming quite interested in what the Thief had to say. Percy fell into Alden's arms, and guilt swamped Chal. These were his friends, and, by asking them to shelter Palmer, he'd brought trouble to their doorstep.

"I'm so sorry, Alden. I should have taken Palmer somewhere else — like one of my safe houses — instead of bringing him here. I didn't think. All I wanted was someone I trusted to watch over him."

Alden rested his hand on Chal's shoulder, giving it a gentle squeeze. "Don't apologise, Chal. You didn't do this. Those bastards Coldston sent did, and he'll be punished for it."

"How can you punish a guy like him? I've done a lot of digging into his organisation, and he's bought a lot of officials off to cover his tracks. I'm sure none of them will want to help Palmer if it means being exposed." Chal shook his head.

Steril rejoined them as the police left to disperse the crowd. Chal took a step back when he saw the anger blazing in Steril's eyes.

"Are you okay?"

The Thief nodded, yet Chal could tell Steril was lying. He took the man's hand in his and tugged him closer. Steril resisted, but finally gave in and leaned against Chal for a moment.

"What's got you so worked up? If anyone should be pissed off, it's Alden. This is his place." Chal turned to look at his friend. "I want you to know I'll replace everything. Order what you need and send me the bill."

"Don't be ridiculous," Alden protested. "You didn't cause the damage, Chal. If anyone should pay, it should be Coldston."

Chal shook his head. "None of this would have happened if I hadn't brought Palmer to you." He looked at Percy. "Make sure he sends me the bills. I have more than enough to cover everything. Now I need to know exactly what happened, so I can go find Palmer. Coldston's more than likely going to kill him."

Alden told his head bouncer, Reagan, to close and get the staff to start cleaning the mess. They headed upstairs to collapse in the living room, except for Steril who paced from one end of the room to the other.

After sitting in one of the chairs, Chal buried his head in his hands and sighed. "I told him he'd be safe here. I shouldn't have promised him anything like that. Everyone's always let him down, and I did it as well."

"Maybe you shouldn't have said he'd be safe, but you know what? You thought he would be, and you brought him to people you trusted. We did the best we could, yet sometimes our best isn't enough," Alden spoke from where he and Percy were curled together on the couch.

"How do I get him back? I wish I could just flash to where he is, grab him, and bring him back to one of my safe houses." Chal grunted. "I should have taken him to one of them to start with."

"How many safe houses do you have?" Percy asked.

"Five or six scattered throughout Catalai. I even have a few out in the countryside. Never know when you'll need to bolt or anything like that. If I get Palmer back, I'm taking him to one of them, and not letting him out of my sight again."

"See what I mean? It's like he's obsessed with Palmer." Alden glanced at Percy. "I've never seen him like this with anyone else."

Chal shrugged. "It doesn't matter if I can't get Palmer away from Coldston. You have to help me come up with a rescue plan."

"Sure. I think we can come up with something." Percy motioned to all of them, even Steril's bodyguards, who Chal had forgotten were in the room with them.

"No."

They turned to look at Steril, who stood in front of the fireplace. His arms were folded over his chest, and his gold eyes narrowed as he stared at them.

"Why not? Or don't you think we can save Palmer?" Chal clenched his hands into fists. While it didn't look like he was panicking, his heart raced with fear that they'd be too late and Palmer would be dead before they could get to him.

All he really wanted to do was race over to Coldston's compound and demand the bastard let Palmer go. Of course, he understood it wouldn't work that way. Yet there had to be something he could do.

"This no longer concerns any of you. The Thieves' Council will take care of Coldston and bring Palmer to the Training Facility. Coldston is keeping a Thief against his will, and the Council will not tolerate that. My father is an arrogant asshole, but he does believe in upholding the laws."

Chal shook his head. "Wait a minute. Who the hell is your father? I'm not going to let you take Palmer somewhere he doesn't want to go. Living in the compound will be just like living under Coldston's control. Palmer doesn't deserve that."

"My father, Jasha Lanicaster, is the head of the Thieves' Council, and one of the most powerful members of the Supreme Council." Steril dragged his hand through his hair and grimaced. "I'm not sure you'll be able to see him, Chal. My father gave very specific instructions when he okayed going in and getting Palmer."

"How long do we have?" A plan swirled in his head. If he had enough time, he could sneak in and steal Palmer away before the Thieves got there.

Steril pursed his lips and thought for a moment. "A couple of hours. It'll take Father time to organise the guards and get permission from the Supreme Council."

"Does he know that some of the Supreme Council is on the take? I know Coldston's bribed several of them for business contracts and to turn a blind eye to some of his illegal enterprises," Chal said, even while he made plans to head to Coldston's compound.

"Yes, he knows, and he knows exactly how to get them to cooperate. You've never met my father, and be glad for that. He's almost as big a bastard as Coldston seems to be, but Father does it for the good of Thieves and his position. Admittedly, he's not a particularly nice man, and tends to be very arrogant about his power, yet I've never really seen him abuse it or take advantage of being who he is."

"Sounds like you have a love-hate relationship with your father," Alden pointed out.

Steril nodded. "Yes. I understand why he does what he does, but it's always been the Council and his position over his family."

Maybe not having any family that cared about him was a good thing, Chal thought. At least he didn't have to worry about whether they loved him or their jobs more. He pushed to his feet.

"I have to go."

"You're not going to rescue him alone."

Alden and Percy both stood. Chal frowned at them and held up his hands.

"I've already caused you a lot of trouble. Things could get dangerous, and I don't want to risk getting you both hurt."

"Thanks for the concern, but you're our friend, Chal, and we've come to think of Palmer as a friend as well. We aren't going to let Steril's father drag the man off to the Facility without giving him a choice." Percy smiled, hooking his arm through Chal's.

"Besides, Coldston knows what you look like, and that will make it difficult to get into the grounds," Alden reminded him.

"True. Which is why I'm coming with you." Steril propped his fists on his hips and glared at them. "He knows what you two look like as well. He won't let you into the grounds either. He'd be afraid you were going to try something."

Chal snorted. "I don't think Coldston gets scared. He's too secure in his own invincibility."

"True, but somewhere deep inside he has to know there will be consequences for what he did. Percy has become well known as Councilman Lobe's right-hand man, since the old guy has decided not to step down yet. He wouldn't let an attack on Percy's partner go unpunished, and, trust me, Lobe can't be bribed by anyone." Steril chuckled. "He's a tough old bird. He and my father have had many shouting matches."

"True, but I'd never go to Councilman Lobe with my problems. I don't want to be one of those people who uses my position for personal reasons." Percy wrinkled his nose in disgust. "I hate people like that. Actually, my father's one of those people."

Chal turned back to Steril.

"Why would you risk making your father angry to help us?" Chal held up a hand to stop Steril from talking. "Not that I don't appreciate the offer, but he'd be pissed off to find out his son disobeyed him."

Steril's burst of laughter was harsh. "I disobey him every chance I can get. I'm doing this because you're my friends, and I want to help. I've never met Palmer, but I think I could get to like him once I do. Plus you're right, Chal. Once Palmer enters the Facility, it'll be a long time before you see him again. It's rare for a Thief in training to get leave privileges."

"I know. It's only after they graduate that they're allowed to leave the compound," Chal said. "Which is why I want to see Palmer before your father makes him disappear for however long it's going to take to train him. I want to make sure he wants this, and doesn't feel like he's trading one cage for another."

Steril walked over to Chal and hugged him. "I get that, and I'll help you. My father's been mad at me before, and he's gotten over it. Let's get going. We'll make our plans on the way over there."

They were all headed towards the door when Chal noticed Steril's bodyguards standing on either side of it. He waved his hand at them.

"Wait. What about them? Won't they try to stop us, or at least call your father to let him know what we're planning on doing?"

Steril chuckled. "No. They're friends of mine, and not my father's men. They'll help us while doing their best to keep me safe."

Chal eyed both Beasors and they nodded, reassuring him they would do as Steril said. He wasn't a hundred per cent sold on the idea of them coming, but he did know Steril couldn't come without them. His friend wanted to help them out, no matter what the consequences ended up being.

They trooped down to the street and flagged down two sleds. Alden had grabbed Reagan and one of his other bouncers to go along with them, in case they needed more muscle. The four of them took one sled while the guards and bouncers took the other.

It wasn't like they were going to try to get away from Steril's friends. Chal had to trust that Steril was right about them helping out. Once they were settled in the seats, Steril turned to look at Chal.

"I'll go in and tell Coldston I'm looking for Palmer. All Thieves need to be registered with the Council, and I'll let him know that I've been informed he has an unregistered Thief in his house."

"Should we have been worried about that when we let Palmer stay with us?" Percy frowned.

Steril chuckled. "No. You weren't going to use Palmer for work or anything. The only time it's important is if you were going to have him do something for you."

Chal crossed his arms and leant back against the seat. "How are you going to convince Coldston you have the authority to see Palmer? You don't exactly look like you're old enough to hold such a position."

"For Thieves, it's not how old you are but how powerful you are that determines your rank in our society. I happen to be very powerful, even though I don't like to use my magic. So I'm one of many who have been authorised to register Thieves who have been flying under the radar." Steril dug out a tablet from his pocket and tapped the screen, holding it up for them to see.

On the screen was a virtual badge and ID stating that Steril Lanicaster was a registrar for the Thieves' Council. Chal grunted, still not convinced it would be enough for Coldston to allow Steril inside. Yet it was the only chance they had, since the bastard knew what the rest of them looked like.

"Once Palmer is brought to me, I'll tell them that I need to take him with me to the Training Facility because he obviously hasn't been trained properly." Steril sounded like he was repeating something he'd memorised. "Coldston can't argue with me because he knows the law, and, if he refuses me, I can charge him with breaking it."

"It won't stop him." Chal was pretty sure Coldston thought he was above the law.

"It will get Palmer out of the compound while Coldston calls his lawyers to figure out what he can be charged with. Once he's out, you whisk him away for a day or two, but I need you to bring him back, Chal."

Chal fought back the instant 'no' he wanted to shout. While every instinct in his body wanted to keep Palmer to himself and protect him, Chal knew Steril was right. Palmer needed to learn how to regulate his power the right way. Being self-trained was all well and good, but there were rules he'd need to know about.

"Give me a day or two to talk to him, to let him know what he's in for by going to the training compound. I don't want him to think I dumped him somewhere. Also, he knows a lot of stuff about Coldston's illegal businesses, so you might want to take him to the Supreme Council, and see if they'll listen to him."

Silence filled the sled while Steril mulled over what Chal had said. Finally, the Thief nodded.

"Okay. You have two days. Make damn sure you keep Palmer safe, and out of sight. Then call me and I'll arrange to meet you somewhere. I'll be the one to take Palmer in, so at least he'll have a familiar face while he goes through the whole process."

Chal sighed softly. "Thanks, Steril. I know this could get you in a lot of trouble, and, while I don't want that to happen, I can't allow Palmer to get shuttled from one prison to another without knowing why he needs to be there."

The sled stopped in front of an imposing iron gate. After climbing out, Steril gestured for his guards and the bouncers to join him. Chal forced himself to stay in the sled. It would blow everything if he jumped out and raced across the lawn into the house, demanding to see Palmer.

The gate opened and Steril walked on up to the house, with his small army of guards. Chal tensed when the front door opened, and Steril, along with his entourage, disappeared inside. His nerves started getting worse the longer Steril was gone, even though he knew it had only been a minute or two since they'd arrived.

Percy rested his hand on Chal's knee. "It'll be all right. It takes time. Coldston isn't going to let Palmer go easily. Steril'll have to prove he has the right to meet Palmer and remove him from Coldston's custody."

"I know, but I can't help being nervous. Coldston's killed people before, or he's had people killed. I know he wouldn't risk the publicity involved if he were to hurt Steril, but Palmer doesn't have anyone to throw a fit if he were to disappear." Chal rubbed his sweaty palms on his pants.

Alden reached around Percy and squeezed Chal's shoulder. "Not anymore. You're here for him, Chal, and so are we. Palmer won't be left with Coldston any longer than necessary. If Steril doesn't get him today, then his father will in a day or two."

Chal nodded. "My mind knows that, but my heart is afraid I'll lose him. Hell, I'm going to lose him either way, whether Coldston keeps him or he goes to the Catalai Training Facility."

"True, but at least Palmer will be alive and safe at the Facility." Alden tugged Percy closer to him. "I hated it when Percy moved in with Kiki. I was afraid something would happen to him and I wouldn't be there to keep him safe, but he was alive and I could talk to him whenever I needed. It's the same with Palmer. You might not get to see him, but you'll be able to chat with him."

Chal didn't want to admit his worries weren't about never getting to see or talk to Palmer again. Deep inside, he worried that Palmer would meet someone better at the Facility, and fall in love with him. He was pretty sure the fear was unfounded, but still he did believe there was someone better out there for Palmer.

Chal didn't deserve a guy like Palmer, sweet and innocent, even after all he'd been through.

"I'm not sure I'm going to be able to wait much longer," he confessed, clenching his hands on his thighs.

"You must and you will. If you do something stupid, Coldston just might kill Palmer instead of letting him go with Steril," Percy informed him.

He knew that, and it was one of his other deepest fears. He would have to trust that Steril knew what he was doing.

"We're going to move to the other sled. That way, when Steril brings Palmer out, you can take him out of the city for a few days." Alden patted him on the shoulder.

Chal nodded, letting his friends leave as he freaked out about what was going on inside Coldston's mansion.

Chapter Nine

Palmer grunted as his guards pushed him into the living room. His body ached from the beating he'd received. He should probably be happy he'd only been roughed up, and not raped. He wouldn't put it past Coldston to have had his men do that to try and break Palmer. Maybe that was on the schedule for later, if Palmer kept resisting the man's demands.

"Why the hell does he look like that?"

The sharp anger in the strange voice caused Palmer to look up. His mouth dropped open when he saw another Thief standing in the middle of Coldston's living room, and it was very evident the Thief was pissed off.

The man's gold eyes flashed with fire and his jaw was clenched. Palmer dropped his gaze to the floor, not wanting to be seen as challenging the Thief, even though he knew he wasn't angry with Palmer.

"Unfortunately, Palmer has a drug problem and it makes him combative. My men have to protect themselves," Coldston lied.

"I'm not on drugs, you bastard." Palmer turned to the Thief. "Sir, I'm here against my will. This asshole and his men kidnapped me from a friend's place. Can you help me?"

The Thief's eyes narrowed like he was trying to decide if Palmer was telling the truth or not. After a few minutes, he shrugged.

"I don't really care whether you're an addict or not, and whether you're being held here against your will. What I am concerned about is that you're an unregistered Thief, and that's against the law." The stranger folded his arms and glared at Coldston.

"Now, Registrar Lanicaster, I wasn't aware of any laws about unregistered Thieves. If I had known, I would have taken Palmer down to the Council's headquarters myself." Coldston smirked.

Lanicaster shook his head. "Don't give me that bullshit, Coldston. Every businessman knows the laws and rules regarding hiring Thieves. If you didn't know, your accountant should have told you the stiff penalties involved."

Coldston's upper lip curled, and Palmer could tell the man was getting annoyed. Yet Lanicaster must have been someone important, because Coldston hadn't thrown him out. Palmer looked at the four men standing by Lanicaster's sides. Of course, the man's bodyguards might have had something to do with that as well.

Palmer kept his mouth shut, not wanting to bring any more attention to himself. He wasn't sure why Lanicaster was there, and, while he didn't think it mattered to his freedom, he did like the fact that his presence upset Coldston.

Coldston started to speak, but Lanicaster turned away from him to study Palmer. He fought to keep from squirming under that intense, golden gaze. Yet something that looked like friendship flickered in the man's eyes, and Palmer wondered if maybe his saviour stood in front of him.

"I need to confirm you aren't registered, Palmer, and then we'll discuss what we're going to do with you." Lanicaster held out his hand. "Give me your hand."

Palmer did as the Thief asked, and he tensed when the man pulled a scanner from his pocket, placing it over Palmer's wrist.

"What are you doing?" Coldston asked, edging closer to them.

He didn't get too far because Lanicaster's men encircled them, keeping Coldston and his enforcers on the outside.

"Every registered Thief has a microchip implanted at his wrist for easy identification. Trust me, when a person can steal someone's very appearance, there has to be a way to track them." Lanicaster looked up from the scanner to pin Coldston with his gaze. "I don't have time today, but within the next day or two the Thieves' Council will send another registrar back to check on all the Thieves you use, Coldston. Something tells me there might be a reason why you're so nervous about my presence here."

"Oh, you'll find that all of my employees are registered with the right Councils. I wouldn't dream of breaking the laws like that." Butter wouldn't have melted in Coldston's mouth.

Palmer rolled his eyes, but Lanicaster was the only one to see him. The Thief's lips twitched like he was fighting back a smile. After another minute, Lanicaster put the scanner away. Not knowing what to do, Palmer stayed where he was. Somehow he knew that being next to Lanicaster, and surrounded by his men, was safer than being anywhere near Coldston.

Lanicaster frowned as he looked at Coldston. "Just as I thought. He doesn't have a microchip, so that means he's unregistered. It also means he has to come with me to headquarters where we'll get him on the books."

"I can bring him down tomorrow," Coldston spoke up, annoyance colouring his voice.

Lanicaster laughed, though there wasn't any amusement in his expression. "I'm sorry. Even if you were to bring him down tomorrow, he wouldn't be able to return with you. Usually, an unregistered Thief is an untrained Thief, and we don't allow those either."

"What are you saying?"

"What I'm saying is Palmer has to leave with me today, and he won't be coming back to work for you. He has to go to the Catalai Training Facility where he'll learn how to use his powers the right way."

"Oh, hell no. You aren't taking him away from here. You can't do that." Coldston started to push past Lanicaster's guards to grab Palmer.

Palmer dodged the man's grasping hand and ducked behind Lanicaster. He didn't know the Thief, but already he trusted him far more than he ever had Coldston. Lanicaster propped his fists on his hips and laughed harshly.

"Do you really think you can stop me? I'm not sure you know who I am, besides being a registrar. I'm Councilman Lanicaster's only son, and you'd be in a shitload of trouble if you were to stop me from doing my job."

Coldston paled and backpedalled so quickly Palmer thought he'd fall over his feet while getting away. So

Lanicaster's father was a big deal, or enough of a bastard that even Coldston was scared of him.

"I'm sorry, Registrar. I didn't realise Councilman Lanicaster was your father." Coldston clenched his hands and nodded. "I'm sure Palmer will be fine with you."

"I'll treat him like he was my own brother. Like I'm sure you did while he worked for you." Sarcasm dripped from Lanicaster's words.

Palmer snickered softly. Lanicaster wasn't afraid of Coldston, and it made Palmer feel almost like he was with Chal. The Tramp hadn't ever acted like he was afraid of Coldston either.

"Let me tell you something, Coldston. I meant what I said about sending more people here to deal with you and all the laws you have broken. I'm pretty sure you've done worse than use unregistered Beasors."

Before Coldston could say anything in response, Lanicaster turned and gripped Palmer's elbow.

"Let's get out of here."

Once again, Palmer found himself escorted by four large men. The difference this time was that he walked out of the front door with a slender Thief by his side. The door slammed behind them with a resounding bang and he winced.

Lanicaster chuckled. "Don't worry. He can't get you again, ever. Once you're micro-chipped and signed into the Facility, you'll be free of him."

"How did you know he had me?" Palmer finally blurted out what he'd been asking himself since he'd first seen the Thief and his men.

"Some mutual friends alerted me to your existence and where I might find you. In fact, they're waiting for us in the sled."

Palmer spied the two hover sleds waiting at the kerb as they strolled through the open gates.

"Mutual friends?" He thought about who it might be, since he didn't know many people in Catalai.

"Yes." Lanicaster gestured to the lead sled. "Climb in, and you'll find out who it is."

Palmer hesitated at the door, glancing over his shoulder at Lanicaster.

"Don't worry. I didn't take you away from Coldston to hand you over to someone just as bad. Just remind him he has to bring you back to me in two days. I can't give you any more time than that."

"All right. Hey, thanks, man. I wasn't sure I'd ever get free of him again." Palmer held out his hand to Lanicaster.

The Thief shook it and smiled. "I told you, we have mutual friends, and one of them would have stormed Coldston's compound all on his own if I hadn't come up with a better plan."

Lanicaster slapped him on the shoulder and headed towards the second sled. Taking a deep breath, Palmer stepped into the sled, afraid of who might be in there, yet he knew whoever it was couldn't be worse than Coldston.

"What the hell did he do to you, Palmer?"

Chal's exclamation surprised Palmer and he tumbled into Chal's lap. The Tramp gathered him into such a tight embrace, Palmer almost couldn't breathe. He wasn't going to protest. Chal was holding him, and whatever fears he might have had disappeared. Palmer slid his arms around Chal's waist, breathing the man's scent in, and closing his eyes.

"Oh, honey, I'm so sorry I wasn't there to keep Coldston from taking you. I have to admit, I thought it would take him longer to figure out you were with Percy and Alden."

Palmer shook his head. He didn't want to talk about Coldston or anyone else right then. All he wanted to do was absorb Chal's presence and let the knowledge that he really was free sink in. Chal seemed to understand what Palmer was feeling, since he stopped talking and settled back against the seat.

He didn't know where they were going, but Palmer realised he didn't care. All that mattered was that Chal held him, and he would never have to worry about being a prisoner again. Chal rubbed his hands up and down Palmer's back lightly. Palmer appreciated his gentle touch because his body was really beginning to ache from the beating.

Finally, the sled slid to a stop and Chal urged Palmer out of the vehicle. Palmer blinked, making sure the small ivy-covered cottage in front of him wasn't part of a dream. Chal joined him, gripping his elbow and encouraging him to walk.

"This is one of my safe houses. It's about forty minutes from Catalai, and isn't in my name. If Coldston is so inclined to look for you, he won't be able to find you before I have to take you back to Steril."

"Lanicaster told me to remind you that he wants me back in two days. That's all he could give you," Palmer repeated what the other Thief had told him.

Palmer watched as Chal pressed his hand to the door lock. "Why does your safe house have a palm scanner? Are you a spy or something?"

Chal grunted, but that was all the answer he gave. The door swung open, and Chal motioned for Palmer to enter. Palmer stepped over the threshold and froze.

Whatever he'd been expecting when he saw the outside of the cottage, it wasn't this.

Brightly coloured walls created a stunning visual that somehow fitted with the overstuffed furniture and pillows. The furniture itself was neutral in colour—tans, browns and blacks. Yet it had a very open feeling.

"There's only one bedroom, but I thought you wouldn't mind that." Chal winked. "If you do, I can sleep on the couch."

"Hell no. I have this feeling that these next two days are the last ones I'll have with you for a while, and I don't want to miss out on anything."

Palmer whirled around, encircled Chal's shoulders with his arms and kissed the Tramp. He didn't know which one of them sighed when their mouths touched, but it felt like everything Palmer had ever wished for rested in Chal's kiss.

He moaned when Chal wrapped his arms around his waist and crushed him to his hard body. Chal cupped his ass, fondling his cheeks with firm fingers. Palmer wanted to climb Chal—he wanted to strip right there in the living room and let the Tramp take him. Hell, he'd even beg if he had to.

Chal eased away a few inches. "Easy, honey. Let me lock up and we can head to the bedroom."

Palmer didn't want to stop kissing Chal, but he knew they had to be careful. Coldston might have had them followed, because he was a bastard like that. Palmer stood back while Chal locked the cottage up, tighter than a prison cell. Maybe Palmer should have panicked at that thought, but he found he liked the idea of being locked up with Chal. At least they could focus on the important thing, which was getting to bed and fucking as soon as possible.

The Tramp didn't even mess with lights or anything like that. He scooped Palmer up over his shoulder and carried him down the hall to what Palmer assumed was the bedroom. Palmer gave a rather undignified squeak when Chal dropped him on the mattress. Sitting up, he watched as Chal started removing his clothes.

"You need to get naked," Chal told him. "Or at least get your pants off."

Palmer didn't argue. He tore off the T-shirt he wore, flinging it away. He attacked the button on his jeans, but froze when Chal touched his hands.

"Palmer, what the hell happened to you?"

He glanced down and grimaced at the bruises marring his upper body. There would be more on his legs. He shrugged.

"Coldston wasn't happy that I got away from him twice. He had his men beat me up. You haven't seen the size of his enforcers. There wasn't anything I could do, except hope they didn't hurt me too bad."

Chal sat on the edge of the bed, resting his hand on Palmer's stomach. "Are you all right? Should I take you to the hospital to get checked out?"

"No." Palmer shook his head. "Aside from the bruises, nothing's broken. I'll be sore for a day or two, but it'll be fine. To be honest, it's nothing I haven't suffered before. Living on the streets can be tough."

He finished tugging off his pants, and grabbed Chal's arm, yanking the Tramp down on top of him. Palmer sensed hesitation in Chal's actions, and figured it was probably because of Palmer's bruises. He buried his fingers in Chal's hair, bringing their lips together again. Palmer teased his tongue along the seam of Chal's mouth, and swept in when he opened for him.

Their tongues tangled as they relearned what made the other inhale sharply or moan. Palmer slid his hands down Chal's back, tracing the Tramp's spine to the top of his crease. He caressed the soft skin and Chal shuddered.

Chal inched down Palmer's body, kissing, nipping, and sucking. Palmer appreciated the fact that Chal tried to be gentle because of the bruises, but he wasn't fragile, and the pain from the bruises was minor compared to the pleasure he got from being with Chal. He pinched Chal's ass, and the Tramp glared at him.

"Don't treat me like I'm going to break, Chal. I'm tough. A few bruises aren't going to stop me from getting you to fuck me."

"Fine."

Chal flipped him over on his stomach, and he gasped as Chal slapped his ass.

"Stay right there."

Palmer huffed in annoyance when he felt Chal leave the bed, but he didn't move a muscle. He blushed a little at the picture he was presenting with his ass up in the air like he was offering it to the first taker.

The mattress dipped when Chal returned. Palmer shot a glare over his shoulder at his lover. Grinning, Chal held up a bottle of lube.

"I didn't want to have to stop right before the really good stuff, and go in search of it." Chal dropped the bottle next to Palmer. "Now where was I?"

He shook his butt. "You were going to do something to my ass."

"Oh right."

Chal leant forward and bit one of Palmer's cheeks.

"Holy shit!" Palmer shouted as the pain mutated into pleasure when Chal licked the injured flesh.

The Tramp chuckled, but didn't say anything else. Chal spread Palmer's cheeks, and breathed a puff of hot air over Palmer's hole. He shuddered while the sensation danced over his nerves. Dropping his head onto his hands, he moaned, letting Chal know how much he actually enjoyed that.

He jumped when Chal licked along his crease, stopping to tease his hole before ending at the small piece of skin behind his balls. He moved his legs farther apart when Chal tapped on one of his thighs, making more room for Chal.

Chal sucked one of his balls into his mouth, and Palmer closed his eyes, twisting his hands into the sheet beneath him. The hot moisture went from one ball to the other until Palmer begged for more. He wasn't entirely sure he could formulate what he meant by more.

The click of the bottle top opening gave him a small warning before lube trickled down his crease. He actually whimpered when Chal rubbed some of the slick over his hole before easing just the tip of his finger inside.

Palmer wanted more of Chal's finger, more of the man's body. Just *more* was all his mind could think at that moment. Chal knew, without Palmer saying a word, what he wanted because he worked in one finger, then pulled out. Palmer considered reaching around and hitting the Tramp, but, just as he was about to let go of his grip on the sheets, Chal pushed two fingers in, along with some lube.

"Yes." Palmer hissed as Chal's invasion burned for a moment before building into pleasure.

He rocked back onto Chal's fingers, helping his lover prepare him for Chal's cock. His own cock stiffened and he wanted nothing more than to touch himself and jerk off, but he didn't want to come until Chal filled him.

"Chal, please. I need you," he pleaded.

Chal smoothed his hand over one of Palmer's cheeks. "Just a little longer, honey. I don't want to hurt you."

"You won't. I need you inside me now."

He shoved back hard, and somehow Chal nailed his gland with his fingers. Pre-cum dripped from Palmer's cock, and sweat covered his skin. Finally, Chal left off tormenting Palmer, and he heard the click of the top on the bottle again.

Resting his forehead on his folded arms, Palmer took a deep breath and relaxed, knowing he'd soon be getting exactly what he wanted. After positioning his cock at Palmer's hole, Chal gripped his hips and started taking him. There wasn't any hesitation or stopping until Chal had buried his dick as far into Palmer as possible.

They both froze as each savoured the sensations of being so intimately connected it was hard to tell where one ended and the other started. Eventually the need to fuck grew too strong, and Chal slipped out. Palmer's protest died in his throat as Chal slammed back in. Soon Chal was hammering into him, driving grunts and soft cries from Palmer.

"Yes. Harder," Palmer encouraged his lover, bracing his hands on the mattress as best he could, so he could meet each of Chal's thrusts with his own action.

The perfect rhythm they'd begun with slowly deteriorated as their climaxes built under their skin. The room filled with groans and moans along with the scent of sweat and sex. Palmer balanced on the edge, not able to take that final leap over into the abyss. At least not until Chal wrapped his hand around

Palmer's cock and squeezed it once before loosening his grip enough for Palmer to slip back and forth.

The added friction was just enough to push Palmer over and he cried out as he came, spilling his cum all over the bed beneath him. Chal pounded into him a few more times before he came, flooding Palmer's inner channel with his hot seed. Palmer tightened his muscles, trying to milk the last drops of cum from Chal.

When his arms gave out, Palmer grimaced as he landed in the wet spot, and his breath rushed from him as Chal collapsed on top of him. As much as he liked to be surrounded by his lover, Palmer couldn't breathe. He lifted one shoulder, hoping Chal got the hint.

"Sorry," Chal muttered and rolled to one side, allowing Palmer to take a lungful of air.

"It's all right. Wasn't able to breathe for a second."

Palmer scooted out of the wet spot and closer to Chal, wanting to snuggle, but Chal climbed out of bed. He frowned up at the Tramp.

"Come on. Let's clean up and change the sheets. At some point, we should put a towel down or something, so no one has to sleep in the wet spot, and we're not having to change the bedding all the time."

"Unless one of us sets out to seduce the other, I don't think we're inclined to plan that far ahead."

He took Chal's hand, and let him tug him out of bed and over to the bathroom, where they cleaned up. When they'd finished, Chal grabbed clean sheets while Palmer stripped the bed. He remade it, and Chal took the dirty sheets to throw in the washer.

"Do you want something to eat, or do you think a nap sounds good right now?" Chal asked as he came back in.

Palmer yawned. "A nap sounds great—I didn't get a lot of sleep last night. Coldston was determined to teach me a lesson by beating the shit out of me."

"I'm sorry it took us so long to get you out of there. Steril said we had to wait a day, and he was going against his father's direct orders. His father was coming to get you. Only it would've taken several days for him to get permission from the Supreme Council."

Chal climbed under the covers and held out his arms. Palmer joined his lover, and let Chal pull him closer. He loved how warm Chal was, and how safe he felt being held by him.

"I didn't get a lot of sleep either. I was worried we'd be too late, and Coldston would either have killed you or he'd have moved you somewhere we wouldn't be able to find you."

He patted Chal's chest. "I had no doubt that you'd figure out a way to save me. It might sound strange, since we haven't known each other that long, but I trust you to keep your word. You promised you would ensure I was safe from Coldston, and you're doing it."

"But I'm not sure if you'll think that. From what Steril says, being at the Training Facility is a lot like being in prison, and that's how Coldston made you live for so long." Chal frowned.

Palmer chuckled. "Trust me, no matter how bad the Thieves' compound is, it can't be anyway near as bad as Coldston's. At least I know they won't kill me if I choose to leave."

"I don't think they'd do that. Someone would've complained sooner if they did," Chal joked.

"See, training doesn't scare me. Will I be able to see you while I'm there?"

Could he admit to not wanting to lose contact with Chal? If someone had asked him even a month earlier, he'd have said he didn't believe in love at first sight — that it was a myth perpetuated by dreamers and fools. Yet from the first night he'd dreamt of Chal he'd loved the Tramp, though he wasn't ready to say anything. He worried Chal might not feel the same.

Chal's shoulder moved beneath Palmer's cheek in a shrug. "I'm not sure. I don't think we'll be able to see each other in person for a few months, but I think we can talk on the phone as often as we'd like. We can check with Steril."

"But not right now. I want to take however many days we've been given for just the two of us."

Chal manoeuvred him around, so that Palmer was on his back and Chal was looking down at him. The Tramp trailed his finger over Palmer's nose before leaning down to kiss him.

"Don't worry. Steril told me we had two days, and I plan on making the most of them before we go back to Catalai."

The emotion in Chal's brown eyes touched Palmer's heart. If the Tramp didn't love him, it looked like he was on the verge of it. Palmer would do all he could to get Chal to love him before he had to leave for training. Palmer had a feeling it would be the only way he could get through the next several months.

Chapter Ten

"It's time," Chal said while they lay in bed, stroking his hand up and down Palmer's arm.

"I know, but I don't want to let you go." Palmer pushed up on his elbow to look into Chal's eyes. "I want to stay here and hide away forever."

"It'd be nice, and I have the money to do it, but I can't let Steril down like that. He risked making his father angry and getting in trouble with the Thieves' Council as a whole by helping us." Chal sighed.

"And he's your friend. We can't let him take the brunt of the problem." Palmer leant down and brushed a kiss over Chal's lips. "Call Steril and set up a meeting place. I'm going to take a shower."

"All right."

Chal watched his lover climb out of bed and stroll into the bathroom. He waited until the door shut behind Palmer before grabbing his phone off the nightstand, and dialling Steril's number.

"Hello." Steril's voice came over the speaker, but nothing came up on video.

"Can you talk?" Chal wasn't going to go into any detail when there might be someone with Steril.

"Let me call you back. I'm in a meeting right now, and can't really chat."

"No problem. I'll be near my phone."

He hung up, and, after letting the phone drop on the blanket next to him, stared up at the ceiling. The past two days had been the best of Chal's life. He and Palmer had spent the time talking, making love and growing closer. He only hoped the closeness would last while Palmer was at the Facility.

The shower started, and Chal resisted the urge to join Palmer under the water. It would be nice, but it would also cause them a delay in facing the outside world. His thoughts drifted, and he remembered what Palmer looked like with water cascading over every inch of his body.

The phone rang as Chal was getting to the best part of Palmer's anatomy. He snatched it up, and checked the ID. It was Steril.

"Hey, there," he answered.

"Sorry about that, but I was talking to my father, and I didn't want him to know you were calling me." Steril sounded annoyed.

"Are you in a lot of trouble?" Chal sat up, bunching the pillows behind him to lean on.

Steril snorted. "No more than usual. Father isn't happy, but there's nothing he can do about it. He'll be less unhappy when I bring Palmer to the Facility."

"That's what I'm calling about. We need to set up a meeting, so Palmer can turn himself over to you." His voice cracked.

"I wish there was some other way, Chal, but I don't see it at the moment. This is the best way to keep

Palmer safe from Coldston, and get him the training he needs."

Chal grunted, but didn't comment on that. "Where do you want to meet?"

He heard the shower turn off.

"How about Alden's place? He wanted to talk to you about the pub anyway," Steril suggested.

Chal nodded, then realised he didn't have the video screen on. "Sounds good to me. We can be there in an hour."

Steril sighed. "That'll work. I can finish up my meeting with my father before coming to see you."

"Is he angry at you?"

The bathroom door opened, and Palmer walked out. The Thief smiled at Chal while tugging on his clothes. Chal frowned, unhappy that Palmer was covering up his gorgeous body.

"He's always angry at me," Steril said. "I'm not particularly worried about it. I have to get back. I'll see you later."

"Bye, Steril."

He hung up and tossed his phone onto the bed. Palmer came over and sat next to him.

"How long?"

"We have to be at Alden's in an hour. Steril will meet us there. He's actually meeting with his father right now."

Palmer grimaced. "That can't be pleasant."

Chal climbed out from under the covers and dressed. He gestured for Palmer to follow him. They went out into the living room and Chal ordered a sled to come and pick them up.

"It probably isn't, but I'm starting to get the feeling Steril isn't letting it bother him anymore." Chal dropped onto the couch. "It's not like he's never going to bring you to the Facility."

Palmer joined him, resting his head on Chal's shoulder. Chal slid his arm around the Thief, pulling him closer.

"I know why I have to go to the Facility, but I can't help wishing I didn't have to."

Chal brushed a kiss over Palmer's temple. "I know, honey. I feel the same way. I've considered grabbing you and running away, but I don't want to get Steril in any more trouble. Also, you do need to learn how to replenish your power after using it."

Frowning, Palmer leant back enough to meet Chal's gaze. "Replenish my power? What do you mean?"

"When you use your magic to steal something, you're tired afterwards. For me, I can flash several times before I need to meditate and rebuild my strength. Every magical Beasor has to do it."

"Really? I don't remember ever being tired after one of my stealing episodes," Palmer murmured.

"Maybe you didn't notice."

Chal's phone beeped, letting them know the sled waited outside for them. After standing, he offered Palmer his hand to help him off the couch. Without talking, they left. Chal locked the cottage and they went to the road, where the sled hovered.

Palmer climbed in first, and Chal followed. Chal entered Alden's address and swiped his card to pay. Once they were on their way, Chal turned to Palmer, and smiled.

"It's going to be difficult, but I want us to keep in touch. I really like you, Palmer. Hell, I might be falling in love with you."

He took Palmer's hands in his and held them tight. Chal stared into Palmer's golden eyes.

"Some may say it's too soon. We haven't known each other for long, and they're right. I don't care. I've decided time doesn't matter when it comes to love."

Palmer studied him, and Chal licked his suddenly dry lips, waiting to hear what Palmer had to say.

"You're right, Chal. I don't want to let go of what we have. I'm afraid we'll lose it if I go to the Facility. I do love you, Chal, with no doubts or questions."

Chal swept Palmer into his embrace, their lips crashing together with all the promise and hope of their love. They embraced, and Chal wished they had time to make love once more.

Yet maybe it was best that the last time they'd been intimate had been in the cottage. Chal knew he'd never sell the place where he'd fallen in love.

"When you're done with your training, we'll go back to the cottage. Maybe we could live there," he spoke aloud.

"Sounds good to me," Palmer whispered.

They held each other, whispering and making plans for what they would do once Palmer had graduated from the Facility. They had no real idea of how long it would take for Palmer to complete his training, but Chal didn't care how long he'd have to wait. He'd work and keep busy, and count the days until Palmer could be with him every minute.

The sled chimed as it pulled to a stop in front of Alden's pub. Chal hugged Palmer and, with every atom in his body, fought the urge to tell the sled to drive back to the cottage. It was silly, really. Palmer wouldn't be in danger once he was in the Facility. Not even Coldston would have the nerve to try to kidnap Palmer from there.

He opened the sled door and stepped out, turning to help Palmer. He didn't pay attention to the people moving around them. Palmer joined him on the sidewalk, and Chal started to head inside.

"I should have known you were behind all this, Farnsmith."

Chal whirled to see Coldston standing a few feet away, fury in every line of the man's body. He pushed Palmer behind him, silently urging him to get inside the pub.

"I don't know what you're talking about, Coldston." Chal took a step back.

Steril was in the pub, and that would mean his guards would be there as well. They'd be able to keep Coldston from trying anything.

"All this bullshit about unregistered Thieves, and sending that imposter to my house to get Palmer. I bet he's not even related to Councilman Lanicaster." Coldston moved closer, with his four huge enforcers behind him.

"I still don't know what you're talking about, but you should probably read the laws again, Coldston. I'm pretty sure most of your business breaks some law along the way." Chal straightened, not willing to give any more ground to Coldston. "It was only a matter of time before the authorities caught up to you."

Coldston snarled and reached out for Palmer. Chal knocked his hand away, and dodged one of the enforcers.

"You're not taking Palmer again. Trust me, the Thieves' Council does want him, and they're waiting to take him away. If you interfere, you'll get into even more trouble."

He heard the door behind him, and while he didn't know whether it was opening or closing, he didn't care. All he wanted to ensure was that Palmer stayed away from Coldston.

"I told you, I don't believe any of the shit that registrar said to me," Coldston shouted.

"You should have. My son may be many things, but a liar isn't one of them."

The icy voice coming from behind Chal caused both of them to freeze. Chal swung around to come face to face with one of the most beautiful Thieves he'd ever seen. Yet the man was also the most intense looking Beasor Chal had come in contact with. He had to be Steril's father.

"Councilman Lanicaster." Chal bowed his head.

While he might not have much respect for his own Councilman, he did respect Lanicaster. The man was in a position to become the next Chairman of the Supreme Council. It didn't pay to piss the man off any more than he already was.

"Tramp Farnsmith, I do believe you were bringing someone here to meet with me today. I appreciate you taking the time to retrieve Thief Holmes for me."

"You're welcome, sir." Chal swallowed.

Coldston cleared his throat, and Lanicaster turned his icy gaze on him.

"Is there something I can help you with, Mr Coldston?"

"I would like to make my case."

Coldston edged closer to Chal, but he eased away, not wanting the bastard near him.

"You'll be receiving a summons to appear before the Supreme Council, Mr Coldston. I suggest you bring your lawyer, and also be prepared to have all of your businesses scrutinised. I'm afraid some people have been lax in their dealings with you. I won't be." Lanicaster's smile struck fear into Chal's heart, and he wasn't even the one it was pointed at.

The Thief looked back at Chal. "If you'll join me inside, Tramp Farnsmith."

"Yes, sir."

Chal scurried ahead and held the door open for Lanicaster to stroll through. He shot a glance back at Coldston, biting back a smile when he saw a group of Thief enforcers blocking the entrance to the pub.

"Mr Coldston has done enough damage to this place, I don't think he needs to return at the moment."

After shutting the door, Chal searched the main room of the pub, and spied Palmer standing with the others near the bar. Forgetting everyone else in the room, he rushed across the floor and embraced Palmer, holding him close. Palmer trembled and laid his head on Chal's chest.

"That was too close," Chal murmured. "I don't ever want to risk Coldston getting his hands on you again."

"Once Thief Holmes has told the Supreme Council everything he knows about Coldston's enterprise, and hands over the proof he has of said infractions, I'm sure there will be no need to worry about him."

Chal stiffened and let go of Palmer, but he kept Palmer's hand in his. He wasn't going to stop touching Palmer until the Thief left. They turned to meet Lanicaster's gaze. The older Thief studied them for a moment before turning to pin Steril with a chilly glance.

"I see you were right when you said Thief Palmer would be meeting you here."

Steril met Chal's questioning gaze with a shrug. "Sorry. He wouldn't stop badgering me about it, so I finally just told him you were going to be here."

"I'm glad you did. If Councilman Lanicaster hadn't been here, Coldston would have caused a bigger scene, and none of us needs that at the moment."

"True." Lanicaster gestured at Palmer, beckoning him closer. "Now, I want to talk to you about why you weren't registered when you were born."

Palmer squeezed Chal's hand once before letting go and walking over to Lanicaster. "I can't tell you why my parents didn't take me in."

"Are they still living?" Lanicaster sat in one of the few chairs scattered around the place, and motioned for Palmer to take the other one.

Palmer did, and the others found places to sit within earshot. Chal didn't care what Lanicaster thought or wanted. He slid his chair right next to Palmer, laying his hand on Palmer's thigh. Lanicaster lifted an eyebrow at the display, but didn't say a word.

"I don't know, sir. They abandoned me when I was ten. I haven't seen them since," Palmer stated.

Lanicaster frowned. "They abandoned you? That's not something any Beasor should do to their child. Our children are our most precious commodity, especially magical ones."

Steril made a choking sound, and Chal wondered if it had been the first time he'd ever heard his father say something like that.

Lanicaster didn't even look over at Steril. "I know my son doesn't believe me, but it was how I was raised, and I would never have left my child on the street. If they are registered, I'll track them down, and they will be punished for not complying with the law."

Palmer shrugged. "It doesn't matter to me what you decide to do to them, Councilman Lanicaster. I haven't thought about them since they left me."

"True, but they still need to be taught a lesson. They left you ill equipped to take care of yourself. You could have drained your power to the point where you died, or went insane. It is irresponsible of your parents to not get you training." Lanicaster shook his head.

"Not everyone is as obsessed with duty as you are, Father," Steril snapped.

Lanicaster grimaced, but Chal couldn't tell if it was because Steril had told the truth or because he'd said something like that in public. There was a great deal of tension radiating between Steril and his father, yet Chal didn't doubt Lanicaster cared for his son. The man just didn't seem able to show it well.

"That might be true, Steril, but if they no longer wanted the responsibility of raising a child they should have taken him to one of the orphanages. Those places don't replace a loving family, but they are still better than leaving a child to fend for himself on the street." Lanicaster drummed his fingers on the table, seemingly lost in thought.

Chal tried hard not to fidget, knowing there wasn't anything he could do. Councilman Lanicaster was in charge of Palmer's life for however long it would take to train him. As annoyed as Steril was by his father, Chal couldn't help thinking Palmer was in the best hands. Lanicaster didn't seem to be the kind of man who could be bought or frightened into doing what Coldston wanted.

"We'll deal with your parents later. Now I want you to tell me everything you know about Mr Coldston. How you met, and what he's been having you do for him." Lanicaster waved one of his entourage over. "We'll tape the whole conversation, but you'll still have to go before the Supreme Council and tell them everything as well."

Palmer looked over at Chal, and he nodded.

"It's the only way to keep you safe from Coldston, honey. Once all the right people know, Coldston has no reason to go after you anymore."

Lanicaster leant forward, and patted Palmer's hand. "All your friends can stay, if you wish. They are my son's friends, so I guess they can be trusted. Even if they convinced him to lie to me."

Chal started to say something, but Steril jumped into the conversation.

"It was my choice, Father. They didn't ask me to do any of this. They're my friends and if I can help them in any way I will." Steril folded his arms over his chest and glared at Lanicaster.

"I know, son, but while I'm glad you have good friends like these, I'm not happy that you lied to me. I have the right to be angry with you, not just as your father, but as the Head of the Thieves' Council. If you can't tell your father, then you should know it's breaking the rules not to tell the Head of your Council."

"Palmer needed to get out of there. He couldn't wait until all the procedures were followed and requests were submitted. I wasn't going to let Coldston hold him prisoner again." Steril jumped to his feet and paced. "Why can't you trust my judgement once in a while?"

Lanicaster followed Steril's path with his gaze until he sighed. "This isn't the place to discuss it, Steril. We'll talk about it again when we're alone. At the moment, I need to talk to Palmer about what he's been through."

Steril clenched his hands. "Yes, sir."

"Thank you." Lanicaster looked back at Palmer. "Now, Thief Holmes, shall we begin?"

Palmer took a deep breath before nodding. Chal wasn't sure he was ready to hear all the things that went on in Coldston's operations, even though he could guess at most of them. He rubbed Palmer's knee, letting his lover know he was there for him.

Over the next two hours, Palmer spoke, telling Lanicaster and the others every detail of what he knew about Coldston and all his illegal activity. He spoke of Thieves stealing people's souls and identities, so Coldston could make money or ruin an enemy. There were Tramps who transported items and people under the radar of the proper authorities, and Gypsies who helped Coldston win horse races and get crops to grow when droughts stopped anything else from surviving.

Alden brought over a glass of water when Palmer stopped to cough. While he sipped, Chal made a decision.

"Councilman Lanicaster, may we break for some lunch? We haven't had anything to eat today."

Lanicaster pursed his lips while he thought, and Chal waited, trying to figure out what was so difficult about the question. Finally, Lanicaster nodded.

"I think that would be a smart idea. There's a deli across the street that's pretty good. At least, Steril's guards rave about it all the time."

"It really is the best around, sir," Percy spoke up. "We can order and some of the men can go pick it up."

Lanicaster gave his permission and, after everyone had ordered, Chal grabbed Palmer and dragged him back to the office.

"I'll bring him back when the food gets here," he promised everyone.

He slammed the door shut behind them, blocking everyone out. Palmer flung himself at Chal, and Chal's back hit the wall. He encircled Palmer's waist, holding him tight and whispering soothing words into his ear.

"I'm here for you, honey. Just remember that. Nothing you say will change how I feel about you." He stroked his hand up and down Palmer's back.

"I hate having to relive all that shit," Palmer admitted. "It makes me feel helpless."

"But you aren't helpless anymore. You have a whole bunch of people who will stand by you and protect you, if you need us. You're not alone, Palmer, and will never be alone as long as I live."

Chal tilted Palmer's head back and kissed him. He slid one hand into the hair at the nape of Palmer's neck and cupped Palmer's ass with his other hand. They rocked together, as close as they could without getting naked. Chal didn't think Alden would like them having sex in his office, though he was pretty sure Percy and Alden had probably fucked several times in there.

Palmer slipped his hands under Chal's shirt, trailing his fingers over Chal's stomach, and Chal moaned.

"You're not making this easier," he complained.

"I'm not interested in making it easy for you to let me go." Palmer winked and leered. "I want you to ache for me."

He cupped Chal's erection and squeezed it. Chal hit the back of his head on the door, fighting back the almost overwhelming urge to tear Palmer's clothes off and bend him over Alden's desk.

A knock sounded on the door, and Percy called through the barrier, "You better not be having sex. I don't want to think about you two being naked when I'm in there."

"It's not like you and Alden haven't fucked in here," Chal yelled back.

"Sure, but it's his office, and I'm his lover. It's like a law that we have to have sex in there at least once."

"I'm pretty sure you've done it more than once. If I go through the desk drawers, will I find lube?"

Percy snorted, and Palmer burst out laughing. Chal grinned, but moved away from the door so he could open it. The Gypsy stood in the hallway with his arms crossed and foot tapping. His lavender eyes glittered with amusement. He waved them out of the office.

"If it were up to me, I'd let you do whatever you want in there, but Lanicaster doesn't look like he has a lot of patience left. I think he really just wants to get this interview done so he can leave." Percy glanced over his shoulder towards the main area before he leaned closer. "I don't think he frequents places like this very often. He seems more of a private club kind of guy."

"Do you think he goes out and has fun? I bet Steril would say he doesn't do anything except work, and keep an eye on him." Chal wiggled his eyebrows, and Palmer giggled.

"The guys are going over to pick up the food, so get your ass out here," Alden yelled from the front room.

They trooped out to find there were more tables set up for everyone to eat at. Chal settled Palmer at one of them before going over to Alden. The pub owner shot him a questioning look.

"Don't worry. We didn't do anything. Percy didn't give us enough time."

Alden chuckled. "Good. I would've had to have done something drastic to get the image out of my head."

Chal punched Alden in the arm. "That's not nice. Are you telling me neither you nor Percy have ever imagined me naked?"

"We're male, Chal. We've pictured everyone naked, except for family members." Alden coughed. "That doesn't mean we want to fuck them."

"True, but come on, you can tell me. Haven't you ever wondered what it would be like with me in bed?" Chal pushed.

Alden shook his head. "To be honest, no. I've never wondered what having sex with you would be like."

Chal peered at the Beasor. "Really?"

"No, and don't act like I'm sick or something. For a long time, I've only wanted Percy, and picturing someone naked is a far cry from wanting to sleep with them," Alden pointed out.

He had to concede that Alden was right. He'd really just been teasing anyway. Chal wasn't truly interested in whether Percy or Alden had imagined him naked, or thought about fucking him.

"What did you want to talk to me about?"

Alden nodded, grabbing some files off the bar. He shoved them at Chal. "Here's the list of items I need replaced. I got good deals on most of the stuff, but I'm going to need you to do another run to Pillian for Percy's wine."

"No problem. Once Palmer's at the Facility and in training, I'll have all the time in the world to do shit for you." Chal scanned the list and didn't flinch at the total cost. "I can transfer the money into your account, and you can order it all."

Alden shot him a shocked look. "Are you sure? That's a lot of money."

"I'm good for it. My fees are pretty high, and I don't spend half of what I make. Also, I told you I'd pay to replace it all, since it was my fault Coldston came here in the first place."

"I appreciate it, man." Alden hugged Chal.

Chal patted Alden's back once before breaking away and heading back to Palmer. The men sent to pick up the food had returned, and it was time to eat.

Chapter Eleven

Palmer smiled over at Chal as the Tramp joined him at his table. He sighed when Percy set a sandwich down in front of him. Chal took two drinks from Alden as he walked by with a tray full of them.

"The deli really is good. One of the best I've frequented, and I've eaten more places than I can count." Chal bumped their shoulders together. "How are you holding up?"

Palmer shrugged. "I'm fine. It's hard to go over everything again, though."

Chal rubbed Palmer's back, and just the simple touch of his lover's hand soothed Palmer.

"I wish I could help you out—and I just remembered something." Chal turned to search out Lanicaster.

When he found the Councilman, he motioned for him to come over to them. Lanicaster didn't seem happy about being summoned, but he came anyway.

"I have a ton of information on Coldston. I forgot about it, but, when he hired me to find Palmer, I did some research on him and his businesses." Chal paused for a moment before continuing, "I could access my files from here, and put them on a drive for you, if you'd like?"

"What could you give us that our own investigators won't?"

"Will your people hack into his computers to get his bank account numbers? Will they spy on him using his phone and computer?"

Lanicaster looked shocked, and Palmer turned to stare at Chal.

"You can do that?" he asked.

Chal nodded. "Sure. If you're not worried about breaking the rules. I'm sure you can't use this information in a court, but you can use it as a base to start your investigation."

Palmer glanced at Lanicaster. The Thief studied Chal like he was a rather fascinating bug. What was Lanicaster thinking? Was he angry that Chal had broken the law, or was he willing to overlook that one small fact in his quest to get Coldston?

"As much as it galls me to say so, I will accept whatever information you have, Farnsmith. While you're right, and it can't be used in court, it'll still give the Council something to look at." Frowning, Lanicaster shook his head. "I can't believe your Councilman allows you to have a contract like that. For a Beasor to get most of the fee, but not go through his council is very strange. I'd never give any of my Thieves permission."

Shrugging, Chal laughed. "What can he do about it? I'm good at my job, and I think I should be paid what I'm worth. Plus I've been screwed over by too many rich bastards who think that just because they're rich, they're entitled to whatever they want. You're an honest man, for all that you're a Thief, Councilman

Lanicaster. You'd never dream of keeping money that wasn't yours. Not every man is like you."

The Tramp paused for a moment, then continued. "I gather information on all my jobs because you never know when it might come in handy to know everything there is to know about a man. Helps keep them honest as well."

Palmer silently agreed with Chal. It was like Coldston, who truly believed he had the right to ruin anyone's life, simply because he had money and power. Of course, there were rich, powerful men who didn't think that, but Palmer hadn't run into any of them yet. It probably had something to do with how he'd spent a majority of his life on the wrong side of the law.

"Yet there are hundreds of Tramps out there who can do what you do," Lanicaster pointed out.

"True, but none of them are as good as I am, or can go as far as I can during a flash. I've never met a Tramp who can do what I can, and I deserve to be paid for it." Chal turned to poke Palmer. "Eat up. Once you're done, and back to talking to the Councilman here, I'll go grab Alden's computer."

He did as Chal told him, mostly because he wanted to get the telling over with. It was starting to wear on him, and all he wanted to do was grab Chal and run away. Leaving problems behind must run in the family, he thought, considering his parents had abandoned him when he was a child.

Palmer didn't want to know if his parents were still alive or not. Some small part of him that was still the little boy of ten wanted them to be dead. It would explain why they had disappeared in a way that meant he wouldn't hate them. The adult in his head told him they had left him because it was too much work taking care of him. They'd never really struck him as being responsible or mature.

After he'd taken his last bite, Percy came around and collected his plate. Lanicaster returned, sitting at the other side of the table, and his secretary sat as well. The recorder was placed in front of Palmer and he took a deep breath.

"I know this is hard, Holmes, but trust me, we'll protect you, and Coldston won't be able to hurt you. Not even the Council members he's corrupted will be able to help him."

Something in the tone of Lanicaster's voice told Palmer the Thief meant what he said, and Palmer trusted Lanicaster would keep him safe. The man had his own reputation to uphold and it wouldn't bode well for anyone who thought to destroy it.

"Thank you, sir. I know you would do your best to keep me safe."

"Our Catalai Facility is the most secure in the country. Ask Steril." Lanicaster paused and frowned. "Maybe you shouldn't ask Steril. My son has figured out how to bypass the security on several occasions, which is why he now has an escort to keep him safe."

Palmer glanced over to where the younger Lanicaster sat, chatting with Percy and Alden. There were two large Beasors standing close enough to stop someone from attacking him, yet far enough away to give the man the illusion of privacy.

"Umm...didn't his guards help him get me away from Coldston?"

Lanicaster grimaced. "We're overlooking that incident. While it was against my orders, he did it for a good reason."

Not sure what to say to that admission, Palmer kept quiet. Lanicaster looked at his secretary, who nodded, and back at Palmer.

"All right then. Let's get the rest of it on record."

Palmer closed his eyes and centred his mind, letting the rest of the memories pour out, not worried about filtering any of it.

* * * *

A further two hours went by, and finally Palmer came to the end. Sighing, he sat back and met Lanicaster's gaze.

"That's all I know about."

"How close were you to Coldston? It seems to me you had extraordinary access to Coldston's operation. How long were you with him?"

"Since I was fifteen, and up until a few months ago, I did whatever he asked of me." Palmer caught the confusion making its way across Lanicaster's face. "I know it doesn't make sense, but before a few months ago he'd never asked me to take someone's soul. He'd just wanted little things—files, or account numbers."

He pushed to his feet and started pacing. Everyone's attention focused on him, but he didn't notice or care.

"Coldston had other Thieves who were more experienced in stealing souls. I'd never learned how to do that, though I know there's a special way to do it, ensuring the Thief doesn't go crazy from taking another person's life in such a way."

Lanicaster curled his upper lip in disgust. "Yes, there are special precautions one must take before one can do that, but it's against the law for a Thief to do such a thing. Just because we have the power to achieve such a thing, doesn't mean we should take advantage of it."

"Yet there are bad people everywhere, and an evil person with such power wouldn't have a problem using it. Also, Coldston paid them a good amount of money to do it. Of course, he made a shit-ton of cash off them as well." Palmer tucked his hands in his pockets and stared at the floor.

"The money didn't attract you?"

Palmer's harsh laugh startled him and everyone else in the pub. "Sure it did. How do you think Coldston got me to go with him in the first place? I was a street kid, barely surviving from hour to hour. Then this well-dressed man shows up, throwing money around like candy. He tells me I can have as much as he does. All I have to do is come with him."

"You went?"

Chal joined them, but he didn't touch Palmer. He seemed to sense that Palmer wasn't interested in comfort at the moment.

"Hell yeah, I went." Palmer glared at them, including Lanicaster and Steril in his gaze. "Maybe none of you understand what it's like to live on the street, and wonder where your next meal will come from. What would you be willing to do to get enough money for food?"

Percy held up his hand. "Actually, I do have some kind of knowledge. I lived on the streets for a while before Alden found me and offered me a room."

"Fine. So one of you out of this bunch has a clue. I'm not proud of what I did for Coldston, but I did it to live. When he finally asked me to steal a soul, I said no. It wasn't something I wanted to try to do. I'm many things, but a killer isn't one of them."

Chal swept him into his embrace and kissed him in front of everyone. Palmer clung to Chal, not wanting to admit he'd been worried that Chal would turn away from him once he'd confessed everything he'd done.

"Honey, I'm not judging you. I'm glad you did what you did, because if you didn't I wouldn't be holding you right now." Chal let him go and cupped his face. "Nothing that happened before we met matters. All that matters is what happens from here on out."

Palmer drew in a shaky breath, and stepped away from Chal. He turned to look at Lanicaster.

"I'm sorry, sir. I didn't mean to get emotional. I'll be better during the meeting with the Supreme Council."

Lanicaster gave him a dismissive wave. "As long as you're honest, Holmes, it doesn't matter how emotional you get. You did say you have hard evidence about some of what you'd seen and heard, right?"

"Yes, sir. I can tell you where I hid it and you can send someone to retrieve it."

"That would be perfect." Lanicaster stood and stretched. "It's time for us to leave, everyone. We still have several hours of processing Thief Holmes, and registering him into the Facility."

Fear rocketed through Palmer and he whirled to look at Chal. The Tramp hugged him again, giving him strength and the knowledge that Chal would wait for him, no matter how long it took.

They didn't say anything to each other, and Palmer nodded. He straightened his shoulders before facing Lanicaster again.

"I'm ready to go."

"Dear boy, it's not a prison sentence." Lanicaster laughed. "Since you are further along than most

Thieves we get at the Facility, I'm sure it won't take you long to learn what you need to know and you can get back to your life. The classes you'll be taking are more about the ethics and morals of being a Thief, so they won't be that hard."

"I'll be waiting for you, Palmer. Remember that, and I'm sure we'll be able to talk while you're gone." Chal smiled at him. "We'll get through this."

Steril moved over to stand by him. "And I'll be there with you. You won't be alone at the Facility."

"Thank you all for helping me. I never had friends before this, and it makes me sad to think I had to wait this long to find some." He blinked back the tears.

Percy and Alden walked over to hug him goodbye. Steril patted his shoulder and moved off with the others. Chal encircled Palmer's waist, pulling him close. Their lips touched in a gentle kiss, their fledgling love fluttering between them. Palmer was going to be the best trainee at the Facility, just so he could get back to Chal as quickly as possible.

They broke apart, and Palmer squeezed Chal's hand once more before he accompanied Steril and Councilman Lanicaster from the pub. They all climbed into the waiting sleds, and Palmer bit his lip to keep from protesting.

He'd agreed to the training, knowing it was the only way he could get rid of the threat from Coldston. He'd known he'd have to be isolated in a compound with other Thieves while he went through the process. Yet he hadn't realised how difficult leaving Chal would be.

Steril reached over and touched his knee. "Don't worry. You can talk to him tonight after we're done registering you. We don't like face-to-face meetings while Thieves are training, because it's very easy to get distracted from the important stuff. But we don't have a problem with you talking to each other, until you're further along in your schooling."

"I'd like to do some tests, Holmes. Nothing invasive or anything like that. They'll be more annoying than anything else, but I have some theories on why Coldston stuck with you so long and what might be one reason why he's come after you. I think there are a number of reasons why he doesn't want to let you go." Lanicaster didn't look up from the file he studied.

"Yes, sir." Palmer was pretty sure he didn't really have a say in the tests or not, but at least Lanicaster talked to him about it.

"Good. Steril, I think Holmes should room with you for now. After he's been at the compound for a while, we'll see about giving him his own room."

"Yes, Father." Steril rolled his eyes and Palmer coughed to cover up his laugh.

"Don't think I don't know what you're doing, Steril." Lanicaster glanced up.

Steril ducked his head, a guilty expression on his face, and Palmer relaxed. There were a lot of issues between Steril and his father, but Palmer got the feeling there was also a lot of love. It was simply that Lanicaster couldn't show the emotion Steril needed to believe his father cared.

* * * *

They arrived at the Facility, causing Palmer's nerves to start up again. Since he'd dropped out of school at ten years old, he'd never been back to anything resembling a classroom, and he worried he wouldn't be able to live up to their expectations. Not that anyone really had high expectations for him, but, still, he was afraid he'd flunk out or something.

He closed his eyes and brought up Chal's image. The Tramp was smiling at him, and Palmer could see the love shining in Chal's eyes. He just had to keep that thought in his mind. Chal loved him. It didn't matter what he did or whether he finished first in his class or not. As long as he had that, he could get through whatever they threw at him.

After climbing out of the sled, Lanicaster led the procession up to the registration building, and Palmer became overwhelmed with everything. He found himself very glad that Steril and his father stuck close to him.

* * * *

Three hours later, Palmer collapsed on his new bed, flinging his arm over his eyes as he sighed. He listened to Steril moving around the room for a few minutes before sitting on the other bed.

"Thank you for all your help," Palmer muttered.

Steril laughed. "You're welcome, but you might want to take that back after a couple weeks of training."

Palmer grunted. "It can't be any harder than what I've gone through to make it on the streets. My concern is getting it finished as quickly as possible to get back to Chal."

"You two really care for each other, don't you?" Steril sounded shocked.

Sitting up, Palmer looked over at the Thief. "Why do you sound surprised? Do you think I'm not good enough for him?"

Steril shot Palmer a startled glance. "I'd never think that. It's just that you haven't known each other for very long. I've never known anyone who's fallen in love that fast."

"Maybe it happened so fast because we'd been dreaming of each other for a while before we met."

"How does that happen?" Steril asked absently, as he stood and went to the dresser. "Father had some clothes brought over for you, since we didn't really give you a chance to get any before we hid you away here."

Palmer caught the pants and T-shirt Steril tossed at him. "Thanks. I don't really have much. I didn't have any way of taking much with me when I ran from Coldston. I haven't been able to pick anything else up since we got back to Beasor."

He stood and started to get undressed. Steril squeaked before turning away. Palmer chuckled, quickly donning the clothes and picking up his dirty ones.

"It's all right. I'm decent now." Palmer held up the stuff in his hand. "Where do I put these?"

Steril waved towards the opposite wall. "Push that red button and a laundry chute will appear. Toss your stuff into it for the laundry staff, and they'll get it back to you first thing in the morning."

"Can't beat that kind of service," Palmer joked as he did as Steril said.

"It's one of the perks about living here." Steril settled back on his bed, hugging one of his pillows to his chest. "Now, tell me about these dreams."

Palmer curled up on his mattress, bunching a pillow under his head as he faced Steril. "Not much to tell. I started dreaming about Chal probably three months before we actually met. I didn't know who he was until I saw him face to face. They started out pretty simple. I was in some kind of trouble, and kept asking him to help me."

Steril snorted. "Don't need a therapist to explain those for you."

"No. I'm pretty clear on what kind of trouble I was in, but why was Chal in my dreams? I mean, yes, obviously I was looking for someone to save me, but why Chal in particular? And why would he be dreaming the exact same dreams about me?" Palmer shook his head. "It doesn't make any sense to me."

"There are a few professors here at the Facility that might be able to give you an answer to that," Steril suggested. "It's just a matter of whether you want to tell them about it or not."

Palmer thought about it for a moment. "I think I'll wait. I don't really know anyone here except you. I'm not inclined to trust people quickly. Look what happened the last time I trusted someone. I ended up a prisoner of some psychotic asshole."

"But you also trusted Chal, and here you are, free of Coldston and hopefully on your way to a wonderful life." Steril sighed. "At least you'll have someone waiting for you when you get out of here."

Palmer studied the other Thief. "Have you dated anyone, ever?"

"At what point would I have been able to meet a guy and date him? Even when I was sneaking out and going to Alden's pub, I knew I wouldn't have the nerve to chat anyone up. Hell, you've met my father. There aren't many people who'd put up with him to date me." Steril stared at his hands for a minute before he shrugged. "Maybe I should just leave, and go to Earth or someplace where there aren't magical beings.

Maybe I can be an ordinary person for once, instead of Councilman Lanicaster's son."

Palmer didn't know what to say. He wasn't sure encouraging Steril to go to Earth was a good idea. He'd been able to survive there because he'd had a little money and street smarts to get him through. All Steril had ever known was the monastery-like atmosphere of the Training Facility. Sure, he'd rebelled and gone into the city, hitting a pub and making new friends outside his circle, but that didn't mean he was ready to head out on his own. Earth was an entirely different ball game, and not every Beasor was ready to deal with it.

"You should really think it through before you make that kind of decision, Steril," Palmer cautioned. "Earth can be a dangerous place for Beasors, and it's very different from our world."

"I know, but that's what I want. I need a different world where I can just be me, and not have to worry about someone wanting me to steal something for them."

Palmer frowned. "You don't like being a Thief?"

"No." Steril glanced at the clock on the nightstand between the beds. "If you want to talk to Chal, you should call him now. We have to get up early in the morning, so we need to get to bed soon. I'll go down the hall to our study library for a while, since you'll want your privacy. You can use my phone."

He didn't know about that, but he appreciated Steril giving it to him all the same. Palmer waited until the door had shut behind him before grabbing the phone off the dresser. He scrolled through the numbers until he got to Chal's, then he hit send.

"Hey, honey."

Palmer grinned as Chal's image appeared on the video screen. His lover sat on a couch somewhere, and Palmer wished with all his heart that he was there with him, instead of in the impersonal dorms at the Facility.

"Hello, Chal. Steril said I should call you now since we'll be getting up early tomorrow and we need to get to bed," he informed Chal.

"Good idea. How'd the registering and everything go?" Chal looked relaxed, and, in a way, it eased Palmer.

He lifted his left arm and showed the Tramp the small red incision where the doctors had inserted his microchip. "Not too bad. It's all confusing, though, and I'm still not a hundred per cent sure why I need to be here. I've never had any trouble controlling my power, or running out of it either. That's why Coldston used me all the time. His other Thieves always needed to rest."

Chal pursed his lips and Palmer was distracted by the urge to taste them. He would have to deal with being able to see Chal, but not touch him. Not for a while anyway.

"I'm sure your teachers will be testing your power and limits. Maybe it's just you've never reached them. Once you try stealing someone's soul, you might find that you don't have the strength you thought."

"I thought they didn't want you to do that, and I really don't either," Palmer commented.

Chal smiled. "Don't worry. It's something one of the first Thieves came up with to train others, but not to actually kill anyone. I've only heard it talked about, but I've never seen it. Steril might be able to give you a better idea of what to expect. The only thing is, if they find out you're special in some way, it might make your training longer than it would have been."

"Well, I'll try not to be special then. I don't want to be away from you any longer than necessary."

Palmer didn't want to talk about what was coming. He'd find out soon enough. He changed the subject, and he chatted with Chal for another twenty minutes about nothing important before Steril returned.

"I have to go now, Chal. I guess morning comes early here." He cleared his throat, suddenly reluctant to say goodbye.

"I love you, Palmer, and we'll talk as soon as you get a moment free."

"I love you too," he whispered before hanging up.

Steril didn't say a word as he showed Palmer where the bathroom was and they got ready for bed. After slipping under the covers and turning the lights out, Palmer stared up at the ceiling, trying not to let his thoughts freak him out.

He had to stop worrying about everything. He'd gone through hard times before, and this was just another bump in the road. He'd do what he had to do, remembering this time that there was someone waiting for him on the other side.

Chapter Twelve

Four months later

Chal paced the main dance floor of Alden's pub, hands shoved in his pockets to hide the trembling. Shit, he'd never been so nervous in his life. Palmer was due at the pub any minute, and Chal couldn't believe how worried he was.

It wasn't like they hadn't talked in the four months since Palmer had left for training, but this would be the first time they got to hold each other again, and Chal was afraid he wouldn't be able to control himself. All he really wanted to do was drag Palmer from the pub and take him to his apartment, from which they wouldn't emerge for a day or two at the least.

"Will you sit somewhere?"

He whirled to glare at Percy, who leaned against the end of the bar. The Gypsy grinned at him, and Chal felt the urge to smack his friend.

"Or have a drink. Do something to calm your ass down. Damn, I never thought I'd live to see the day where you were tied in knots." Percy gestured for Alden to come over. "Pour Chal a mug of that ale he likes."

Alden brought the mug over to him, and Chal took it, though he didn't really want it. He took a swig, and set it on the bar next to Percy before pacing again.

"What's your problem? Steril called and said they were on their way. It won't be much longer," Alden reminded him.

"I know, but I have this awful feeling in my stomach. What happens if we see each other, and it's not the same as it was in the beginning?"

Percy sighed. "It's not like you haven't even talked to each other over the last months. You just haven't been able to touch each other."

Chal shot the Gypsy a look, and Percy gasped.

"That's the problem. You're going to want to jump his bones the moment he steps in the pub, and you're afraid you're going to make an idiot of yourself because of that."

"I'm an adult, Percy. I can control myself." Chal shook his head. "I don't really know why I'm so nervous. I know he still cares about me, and you're right, we've talked almost every night since he left."

He shoved his hands through his hair and began to pace again. Alden and Percy watched him as he walked, muttering to himself.

"I know he loves me. I doubt he's changed his mind after being away. Yet what happens if he did? Now that he's one of the most powerful Thieves in Beasor, why would he want to be with me? I'm just a Tramp. Sure, I've got money and I'm relatively good-looking, but I don't have anything else to offer. I'm not highly placed in society or anything like that. In fact, most people avoid me."

"Do you really think Palmer is that shallow?" Alden interrupted Chal's tirade.

"No, I don't, but I can't help the way my mind is working at the moment. Nothing like Palmer has ever happened to me before, and I'm afraid he'll come to his senses and bolt. It's the sensible thing to do." Chal gestured wildly.

Alden stepped up to him and grabbed his arms, shaking him hard once. He blinked at his friend, and Alden smiled.

"I thought you were going to have a panic attack or something. Get a hold of yourself, man. It'll be fine, and, once you can hold Palmer again, all your worries will go away. Now Percy and I expect to see you and Palmer at lunch tomorrow. It'll be our treat and at the usual place."

Before Chal could say anything else, Alden swung him around and there stood Palmer right in front of him. Chal didn't think or care about the others in the pub with them. He wrapped his arms around Palmer's waist, and yanked the Thief close. Their lips met in an explosive kiss. Chal wanted to devour his lover and he wanted to get Palmer in bed as soon as possible.

Palmer didn't protest Chal's rough handling as the Tramp waved vaguely at his friends while dragging Palmer from the pub. He grabbed the first sled available, practically shoving Palmer into the back seat. After getting in, he told the computer his address and swiped his card for payment before turning back to look at Palmer.

"I'm glad to see you too," Palmer joked.

"I'm sorry. I didn't even give you a chance to say anything to Percy or Alden." Chal hung his head, ashamed of how he had acted.

Palmer put his knuckle under Chal's chin and lifted his face until they were gazing into each other's eyes. "I'm not complaining, Chal. It's nice to know you missed me so much, you can't think of anything except the two of us together."

Chal took Palmer's hand in his and wrapped his lips around one of the Thief's fingers. He sucked and licked it until Palmer's eyes glazed over with desire and he moaned. Chal smiled and eased up a little, not wanting to get Palmer too hot and bothered.

"It's totally true. All I thought about was dragging you off to my apartment and letting you fuck me until we were exhausted and couldn't move. I've changed my mind."

Palmer frowned. "Okay?"

"We're going to the cottage for the night. Alden told me he wanted to meet us for lunch tomorrow at our restaurant, and we can do that, but I want our first time together after so long to be at the cottage."

"You don't know how many times I thought of our time there, and wished I was there instead of at the Facility." Palmer cuddled into Chal's side. "I'm so glad I got out of there."

"But you have to go back, don't you?" Chal tightened his arm, pulling Palmer onto his lap.

Palmer rested his head on Chal's shoulder. "Yes, that was the agreement. They let me live away from the Facility, and I go back twice a week for more tests. I'm still not sure what they're looking for, but I'm willing to let them do what they want as long as I don't have to stay there any longer."

"I'm happy they agreed to letting you out of the Facility. I really missed you." Chal nuzzled Palmer's temple. "I missed holding you, and sharing a bed with you. Is it strange that we've only known each other for close to five months, yet I can't see my life without you anymore?"

"It's not strange," Palmer said.

"Do I sound like a girl babbling about not wanting to live without you anymore and shit like that?" he joked.

Palmer chuckled. "No. You're saying exactly what I want to hear."

"Good, because I love you, Palmer, and I don't want to spend a night apart unless it's for work."

The sled came to a halt and Chal opened the door, allowing Palmer to climb out first. Once Chal got out and shut the door, he sent the sled back to Catalai. They went inside and headed straight to the bedroom. Without a word, they stripped and climbed into bed.

Chal found the lube and handed it to Palmer. "I want you to take me, Palmer. It's all I've been thinking about since you left."

Palmer's eyes widened. "Are you sure?"

"Yes, I trust you, and I know you won't hurt me. So I want you to fuck me again. Just like you did on Earth."

He stroked his cock, pumping it a couple of times while watching Palmer pop the top off the bottle and squirt slick onto his fingers. Chal hooked one hand behind his knee, bringing it up to his chest, and exposing his hole to Palmer's gaze.

Palmer licked his lips and trailed his fingers down from the base of Chal's cock, over his balls to his opening. Chal bit his lip when Palmer pressed one finger in, breaching the ring of muscle guarding Chal's inner passage.

"Oh," Chal whispered, breathing deep as Palmer pushed further in.

Each stroke in brought a gasp of pleasure from Chal, and soon he was caught up in the sensation of being filled with Palmer's fingers. By the time Palmer had three fingers in, Chal was rocking into them, fucking himself on them. Palmer leaned in and sucked Chal's cock in, surrounding it with heat.

"Holy shit!" Chal shouted.

He arched up, shoving his cock into Palmer's mouth while tightening his muscles around Palmer's fingers. An electric shock raced through him when Palmer hit his gland. Everything pooled at the base of his spine and his cock stiffened.

"I'm gonna come, honey," he warned Palmer.

Palmer tapped his hip, to let him know it was okay. He thrust one more time, and came, flooding Palmer's mouth with his cum. Palmer swallowed before licking him clean. Chal flopped back and grunted.

"Don't fall asleep on me yet," Palmer demanded.

"Okay." Chal waved his hand in Palmer's direction. "Do what you want with me. I'm just going to lie here, and try to catch my breath."

He smiled when Palmer laughed. Closing his eyes, he relaxed and just let Palmer do whatever he wanted.

"Whoa," he said as Palmer grabbed his legs and put them up over his shoulders.

Palmer positioned his cock at Chal's opening and gripped his hips. With one fast shove, Palmer was buried deep inside Chal, his cock filling his inner channel.

Trust was a hard thing for Chal to give, and Palmer had been the first man Chal had ever loved. Loving someone meant giving them everything in his heart, and that meant his ass as well. Yet as they lay there, waiting for Chal to adjust to Palmer's cock, Chal knew he'd give Palmer anything the man asked.

"Are you all right?" Palmer stroked his hand along Chal's hip.

"Yes, I am." Chal clenched his passage and Palmer moaned. "I think you can start moving. If you wanted to."

"Oh, thank God," Palmer muttered.

Chal's laugh turned into a groan when Palmer slipped out and slid back in, pumping gently in and out. His lover held his hips at just the right angle, as he bumped Chal's gland every time he thrust in.

He'd never got hard again so soon, yet Chal's cock slowly stiffened and his balls began to draw closer to his body. The overwhelming feelings caused by Palmer fucking him were bringing him to the brink again.

After placing his hands against the headboard, Chal shoved into Palmer's thrust, and both men grunted as their bodies slammed together. Palmer slowly began to lose his easy rhythm. Soon the sound of skin against skin echoed around them and Chal's climax tingled, making every nerve ending spark as he came, unable to hold back any longer.

Palmer paused for a second above Chal, staring down at him with love in his eyes. Chal couldn't say a word as he rode the waves of pleasure once more, though they were weaker this time.

The Thief buried himself balls deep in Chal's ass one last time before he coated Chal with his cum. It was odd to experience being filled in such a way, since he'd only bottomed once before with Palmer. Yet he'd definitely do it more often.

Palmer pulled out, and crumbled at his side, one arm thrown over Chal's stomach. Their chests heaved, working overtime to bring air to their lungs. Chal lost track of time as he laid there, listening to Palmer breathe and feeling his cum dry on his skin. Finally, he couldn't deal with it anymore. He patted Palmer's hand.

"Let's clean up, then grab something to eat. I'm famished."

Palmer snorted. "Who uses that word nowadays?"

"I do. Now move." Chal pinched Palmer's ass after he climbed out of bed.

"Hey, that's not nice." Palmer rubbed the offended area while glaring at Chal.

Chal leered. "I'll kiss it and make it better later. Right now, I need to eat. I was so nervous about seeing you again earlier, I couldn't eat anything without worrying I'd throw it up."

They washed up before heading to the kitchen. Chal checked the refrigerator, and was glad to see the supplies had arrived like he'd ordered. He hadn't planned on bringing Palmer back to the cottage right away, but he'd figured they would have made it there eventually. He made them sandwiches while Palmer got their drinks.

He led the way back to the bedroom where they sat on the bed and ate. Palmer grinned at him.

"You know I talked to a couple of my teachers about the dreams we had before we even met," Palmer informed him.

"Really? What did they have to say?" He took a sip of his ale.

"They aren't sure what caused it or even how it's possible, though one did say that somehow we managed to connect on a psychic level before we even met. Like it was pre-destined for us to be together."

Chal shrugged. "I don't know about that, but it makes sense in a way, I guess."

He reached over and rested his hand on Palmer's knee. The Thief covered his hand with his own.

"I don't care how it happened. Maybe it was to help me trust you when you finally found me," Palmer suggested.

"Maybe." Chal didn't care one way or the other. All that mattered was they were together right then and there. He wiggled his eyebrows at Palmer. "Why don't we take a nap? Recharge for more sex later on. I want your ass this time."

Palmer blushed, but removed their plates from the bed, setting them on the nightstand. "Sounds like a plan to me."

Chal grabbed the blankets and lifted them, allowing Palmer to slide under them. He joined his lover and wrapped his arms around Palmer's waist, pulling him back against his chest. He placed a kiss on Palmer's neck and sighed.

"I think I missed this most of all," he confessed in a low voice.

Palmer entwined their fingers. "I did as well. It was hard to sleep at the Facility without you there to share my bed, though it wouldn't have been anywhere near big enough for the both of us."

"Then we would've had to sleep closer together. Maybe I could've used you as a blanket." He hugged Palmer.

Palmer chuckled, but didn't reply. They fell into the first restful sleep either one of them had had since Palmer had left.

* * * *

After an early-morning round of lovemaking, Palmer and Chal got ready to head back into Catalai to meet Percy and Alden for lunch. They climbed into the sled Chal had ordered, and settled in for the ride.

Chal cleared his throat. Why was he suddenly so nervous again? It wasn't like he wasn't sure how Palmer would answer. Didn't he know? What happened if Palmer didn't say yes? What would he do then?

He gave himself a mental shake. There was nothing to do but ask, and deal with the outcome.

"I was wondering if you'd like to move in with me," he blurted out.

Palmer blinked and stared at Chal. "Move in with you? Are you sure?"

"Yes, I'm sure. I'd never ask if I didn't want you. You don't have anywhere else to live, and I've discovered I hate not sharing a bed with you at night. Also, I love you, and want to spend every waking hour together, except for when we're working," he confessed.

Palmer's eyes lit up as he threw himself into Chal's arms. "Yes, I'd love to move in with you. I love you too, Chal, and I don't want to sleep alone any longer."

Chal kissed Palmer, sealing their new commitment. They could discuss where they'd live later, though Chal was going to push for the cottage. He'd already sold most of his safe houses, and was in the process of letting his apartment go as well. If Palmer didn't want to live in the cottage, Chal would start looking for someplace else that would be perfect for both of them. After all, he had more than enough money to buy another house or two.

In between kisses, they talked about Palmer's training and what he thought of the training compound. Before they knew it, the sled slid to a stop in front of the restaurant. Palmer got out first, and he joined the Thief on the sidewalk.

"Well, look at the happy couple."

They turned to watch Percy and Alden stroll up to them. They all hugged and went into the building. The hostess sat them at what Chal was beginning to think of as their table. After ordering, Percy grinned at them.

"You two truly look happy. Being in love agrees with you," the Gypsy commented.

"I think you're right, and Palmer is going to move in with me." Chal took Palmer's hand in his.

"That's great news," Alden congratulated them.

Palmer nodded. "While I was at the Facility, I discovered I didn't like sleeping by myself and I hated not being able to touch Chal whenever I wanted. Living together is the best of all worlds. I get to share a bed with him, and spend all my free time with him, if I want."

"Oh, there'll be times when you want to have your own space or not see him for an hour or two," Percy predicted.

"True," Alden agreed. "But it'll only last a little while, then, once you see each other again, you won't be able to remember why you wanted to be alone."

Chal understood there'd be an adjustment period, since Palmer had never lived with anyone else, and Chal had only lived with Weston. He pushed his ex-boyfriend out of his mind. Weston didn't matter anymore. The only person in his life was Palmer, and the Thief was all he needed.

"Oh, we have good news." Percy bounced in his chair.

Alden laughed and patted the Gypsy on the shoulder. "To be honest, I'm surprised he lasted this long before telling you."

"Telling us what?" Chal glanced over at Palmer who wore a puzzled look.

"I assume you didn't read or watch the news this morning?"

"Umm…no. We were doing other things." Chal winked at Palmer.

Percy actually giggled. "I can guess what you were doing. Anyway, they arrested Coldston earlier this morning. Dragged him kicking and screaming out of his mansion. The man was pissed off."

"Of course he was. His whole empire has been taken down by one ungrateful Thief." He squeezed Palmer's hand. "I'm so proud of you for doing what you did."

"Councilman Lanicaster warned me it was going to happen sometime soon. I'll be called into testify against him, but, since I'm not the only witness they found, they're not going to put me in protective custody."

"That's good because I don't want you leaving me again," Chal said.

Palmer leaned into him. "Don't worry. It won't ever happen. You're stuck with me for the rest of your life."

Chal swooped in and kissed Palmer on the lips. "I think I can handle that."

"Palmer, tell me, what did they figure out when they tested you?" Percy changed the subject.

"They found out I'm one of the most powerful Thieves they'd ever seen. Turns out I don't need to rest after using my power. At least, we haven't reached a point where I've been too tired to continue." Palmer fidgeted with his glass.

"I've never heard of that before," Alden admitted.

Palmer motioned vaguely with his hand. "There are a few of us around. Steril is one of them too, but, while I don't have a problem using my power, Steril won't use his at all. He hates the idea of stealing anything."

The other three nodded. Steril had spoken often of how he felt about the entire ethics of stealing and being a Thief. It didn't surprise him the other Thief would be reluctant to use his power.

"But hey, having all that stamina must be a good thing in bed. Could make for marathon sex," Percy teased.

"You're so right," Palmer bragged and leered at Percy. "Are you jealous?"

Alden grunted. "Our love life is perfectly fine, Palmer."

They all laughed, and Chal settled in to spend a marvellous lunch with two of his best friends and his lover. Life couldn't get any better than that.

* * * *

Steril stood outside the restaurant, staring through the window at the table where his friends sat. If he walked in there, they'd welcome him with open arms, and pull out a chair for him to sit. He could join them and not be judged for whose son he was, or what he could do with his powers. They didn't see him as Steril Lanicaster, a powerful Thief and heir to the Lanicaster fortune. No, his friends simply saw him as Steril, a person in his own right, unbound by labels or family obligations.

Yet he couldn't go and join them. They looked happy, like they were celebrating something, and he didn't feel happy or carefree. All he really wanted to do was run away. He wanted to leave his life behind, and become someone else for a while.

After turning away from the window, Steril continued down the sidewalk, trying to think of a way out of the world he'd been dragged into. His father loved all the backstabbing and political intrigue surrounding the Councils and Beasor society. It seemed, at times, to be all his father cared about.

Steril wanted none of that. All he wanted was to be ordinary and live like normal Beasors did. He didn't want to be surrounded by bodyguards and be forced to live at the Training Facility all his life. Jealousy nipped at his heart. Why couldn't he be like Alden? Just an ordinary Beasor who lived his life as he wanted without interference from anyone.

As he strolled, ignoring the men following him, Steril came up with a plan. He had to take control of his life, and do what he wanted instead of letting his father dictate what was going to happen in his life. Steril thought about going back and talking to Chal, but he didn't want to get his friend into trouble. When Councilman Lanicaster found out what his only son had done, he would be furious, and Steril didn't want his friends to get blamed for it.

With his decision made, Steril headed in the direction of the coffee house where he'd get one last cup of coffee and a muffin before he went back to the Training Facility and put his plans into action.

About the Author

There is beauty in every kind of love, so why not live a life without boundaries? Experiencing everything the world offers fascinates TA and writing about the things that make each of us unique is how TA shares those insights. TA lives in the Midwest with a wonderful partner of twelve years. When not writing, TA's watching movies, reading and living life to the fullest.

T.A. Chase loves to hear from readers. You can find her contact information, website details and author profile page at http://www.total-e-bound.com.

Total-E-Bound Publishing

www.total-e-bound.com

Take a look at our exciting range of literagasmic™
erotic romance titles and discover pure quality
at Total-E-Bound.